Blotto, Twinks and the Phantom Skiers

Blotto, Twinks and the Phantom Skiers

Simon Brett

CONSTABLE

CONSTABLE

First published in Great Britain by Constable in 2024

Copyright © Simon Brett, 2024

3 5 7 9 10 8 6 4 2

The moral right of the author has been asserted.

A CIP catalogue record for this book is available
from the British Library.

ISBN: 978-1-40871-658-8

Typeset in Palatino by Photoprint, Torquay
Printed and bound in Great Britain by Clays Ltd, Elcograf S.p.A.

Papers used by Constable are from well-managed forests and
other responsible sources.

Constable
An imprint of
Little, Brown Book Group
Carmelite House
50 Victoria Embankment
London EC4Y 0DZ

An Hachette UK Company
www.hachette.co.uk

www.littlebrown.co.uk

To Philippa and Takashi

1

Finishing Required?

'Winter Sports?' echoed Blotto. 'Tickey-tockey! Of course I know what you mean. Hunting, shooting . . . even fishing if you've got the spoffing patience. Not to shimmy round the shrubbery, you mean the whole sporting rombooley, except for crickers and tenners.'

'That wasn't actually where I was dabbing the digit,' said his sister Twinks.

'You mean you do include crickers and tenners?' asked Blotto incredulously. 'Well, Twinkers, you're very definitely shinnying up the wrong drainpipe there. Crickers and tenners are only played in the summer and—'

'Blotters, Blotters, will you, just for a momentette, lock your lugs on to what I'm saying? I am not putting cricket and tennis into the same eggbasket as hunting, shooting and fishing. The winter sports I'm referring to are flip-madoodles like skiing.'

'Oh, those aren't proper sports,' objected Blotto. 'The people who do those live . . .' he loaded the word with maximum contempt '. . . abroad.'

'Some boddoes ski in Scotland,' his sister pointed out.

'Well, that's spoffing well abroad!' said Blotto, with all the certainty that would be possessed by any right-thinking upper-class Englishman. Though he enjoyed porridge and kippers as components in his huge break-fasts, and would never say no to a large whisky, Blotto was properly suspicious of people who played bagpipes and wore skirts. He was equally suspicious of Scotland's so-called aristocracy which, in his view, were at least as tonky as their Irish equivalents.

Brother and sister were sitting over cocoa in Twinks's boudoir, an oasis of lace and white silk nestling within the medieval stone austerity of Tawcester Towers, the ancestral home of the Lyminster family, which had been built soon after the Norman Conquest. The current Duke of Tawcester was the siblings' older brother, universally known as Loofah. (The Lyminsters belonged to that level of the aristocracy where it was thought rather bad form for nick-names to have any relevance. They should be scattered randomly, like confetti.)

Though Loofah was nominally in charge, no one doubted that all affairs of the stately home and estate were run by their mother, the Dowager Duchess. She had worn the patrimonial trousers while her husband was alive, and saw no reason for a detail like his death and the passing of the title to their elder son to make any change to her habits.

'Anyway, Twinks me old tooth-powder-box,' asked Blotto, 'why are you suddenly cluntering on about skiing?'

'Because, Blotto me old trouser turn-up, I want you to join me in an excursionette to Switzerland.'

'"Switzerland"?' echoed her baffled brother. 'But that's abroad.' The final word was, once again, marinated in centuries of xenophobia.

'You're bong on the nose there, Blotters!'

2

'Then why, in the name of snitchrags, would you want to go abroad?'

'Because, brother mine, the Mater is of the view that I need to improve my marriage prospects.'

'Toad-in-the-hole, Twinks! I didn't think you wanted to tie the old reef-knot for a while yet.'

'I don't, Blotters, but the Mater doesn't know that. Did the gin-gen ever trickle into your brainbox that there are Jereboamsful of finishing schools in Switzerland?'

'I have heard of such establishments. And met some of their products. Poor little droplets who seemed rather overkeen to get my wrists into the matrimonial manacles.'

'Exactamento, Blotters! Swiss finishing schools stuff young gels up to their necks with desirable assets for the marriage market, rather in the way the foie-gras makers of Toulouse stuff geese with corn. It is my intention to persuade the Mater that such instruction could make me a more marriageable morsel for some predatory duke.'

'But – hate to put a lump in your custard, Twinks me old pineapple-peeler – aren't you a bit over the horizon to be going to school?'

'The finishing school which I am planning to attend – in the village of Luzvimmen – runs a special course for gels with a few more rings round the old trunk.'

'Toad-in-the hole! Does it really?'

'No, of course it doesn't! But the important thingette is . . . that I will tell the Mater it does.'

'Well, I'll be battered like a pudding! So, what is your planette, Twinks me old horseshoe-stone-extractor?'

'My planette, Blotto me old radio valve, is that you and I should pongle off to Switzerland . . .'

'In the Lagonda?'

'Of course in the Lagonda! Is the King German?'

A beam spread across Blotto's handsome patrician features. Along with his cricket bat and his hunter Mephistopheles, the magnificent blue car was one of his most treasured possessions.

'Then,' Twinks continued, 'while I attend my course at the finishing school, you can light up the fireworks of fun with winter sports!'

'It all sounds creamy éclair,' said Blotto.

'It'll be larksissimo!' Twinks affirmed.

'Except, of course,' realised Blotto, to whom things came considerably more slowly than they did to his sister, 'you won't actually be attending your fumacious course at the finishing school, will you?'

'Give that pony a rosette!' said Twinks.

'So, what, sister of mine, will you actually be doing in Switzerland?'

'I'll uncage the ferrets on that one, brother of mine,' said Twinks, 'when the time is right.'

And, for the time being, with that rather minimal amount of information, Blotto had to be content.

In the Blue Morning Room the following morning, the Dowager Duchess of Tawcester looked, without enthusiasm, at her two younger children. Breeding was one of the most important duties of people of her breeding but, once the offspring had been actually born, the parents felt no obligation thereafter to show much interest in them. The level of maternal nurturing shown by mothers in the British aristocracy is comparable to the amount a female frog shows for her tadpoles. Once spawned, ever forgotten.

And the idea of British aristocrats showing affection towards their offspring was positively bad form.

4

Once the succession had been secured, the job was done. And the Dowager Duchess felt she had fulfilled her commission beyond the call of duty in that respect. Her first child, commendably, had been a boy. Rupert – the firstborn in the Lyminster family was always called Rupert – was the 'heir', the one known as 'Loofah'. But, in time-honoured aristocratic fashion, the Dowager Duchess (back then, of course, just 'The Duchess') went through the tedious process of producing a 'spare'. In the form of Devereux Lyminster, the younger son who was seated in front of her that day in the Blue Morning Room.

Some ducal couples would have stopped there. An heir and a spare were traditionally all that was required. What use could a girl possibly be? But the Dowager Duchess, from her own family history, knew the precise answer to that question. By producing a daughter – in this case Honoria, universally known as 'Twinks' – she had created a useful bargaining counter. The sole purpose of such a daughter's life was marriage to someone rich. And the Dowager Duchess had invested considerable effort into achieving that end. Twinks's resistance to being clapped into the marital manacles was a source of constant frustration to her mother. Why could she not have produced a daughter who was more biddable? And, in a classic pot-and-kettle scenario, the Dowager Duchess conveniently forgot how unbiddable she had been throughout her entire life.

So, she was prepared to listen to her daughter's account of a (fictitious) finishing school in which marriageability could be increased. She expressed the hope that the curriculum there included intensive classes in Biddability.

'The subject is rated so highly that there is spoffing

Biddability Cup awarded every year,' Twinks fabricated with practised ease.

'I will be even more disappointed in you than I usually am,' the Dowager Duchess asserted, 'if you do not return from Switzerland with that trophy in your luggage.'

'I'm a copper-bottomed cert to bring it home,' Twinks assured her. 'I'll come back as biddable as a Royal Flush.'

'What I fail to understand at the moment,' the Dowager Duchess went on, 'is why your brother is required to accompany you to foreign climes. Though, of course, I always welcome Blotto's absence from Tawcester Towers . . . and indeed would greatly welcome the news that you will both be away for Christmas.' It was then late November. Because all the resident family were forced to gather together for at least one meal during the season, Christmas at Tawcester Towers was a time of particular grimness.

'Nada problemo,' said Twinks. 'We can put the tin-lined guarantee on missing the mince pies.'

'Excellent,' the Dowager Duchess rumbled with satisfaction.

But Twinks's hopes that her mother might have moved on from asking why Blotto needed to go to Switzerland were quickly dashed, as the old woman continued, 'I cannot, however, see any justification for your brother's travelling with you on an expensive jaunt of pure pleasure . . . particularly given the ongoing drain on the Lyminster finances occasioned by continuing problems with the plumbing.'

(A short digression is called for here, on the subject of the Tawcester Towers plumbing. The expectation of weekend guests in that kind of stately home was that their bedrooms would feature icy draughts and damp sheets, and that the taps in the bathrooms – of which there were far too few – would yield only a tepid trickle of brownish water. This had always been the case at Tawcester Towers, and many of Blotto and Twinks's adventures had been embarked on to raise funds for improvement. But, however much loot they brought back, in the form of gold or diamonds, the costs of the plumbing soon swallowed them up. Even the introduction of a new boiler and radiator system by a crooked plumber called Rodney Perkins had only brought temporary relief. His efforts, and those of an equally crooked hotelier called Ulrich Weissfeder, who had organised a major make-over of the Tawcester Towers interiors, had not had a lasting effect. Once again, weekend guests encountered icy draughts, damp sheets and tepid trickles of brownish water.

And, rather shockingly, aristocratic house guests, mostly through the traffic of marrying Americans, now knew that such low standards were no longer unavoidable. Some had even been known to go completely the wrong side of the barbed wire and complain to their hosts about the plumbing.)

Aware of this history, Twinks had anticipated her mother's reaction to the idea of Blotto going to Switzerland and had her own response ready. 'The fact is, Mater, not to fiddle round the fir trees, that I won't be the only twig off a family tree being spring-cleaned at the finishing school.'

'I don't comprehend your drift, Twinks. I was talking about Blotto.'

'My drift is, Mater, that the finishing school attracts many shrimplets of the right background like myself, scions of the gentler gender, whose parents are as desperate to get them off their hands by twiddling the marital reef-knot as you are with me.'

'So, you are suggesting . . . ?'

'I am suggesting, Mater, that, as these "finished" debs roll off the production line, with their marriageability and biddability freshly enhanced, the pick of the punnet could be appropriated by a younger son who was actually on the spot.'

'Ah.' The ancestral head nodded slowly. 'I think I see the direction in which you are wending.'

Twinks finished the thought for her. 'Just in the same way that I'll be more likely to ding the church bells with someone after the "finishing" process, Blotto will be right on the prems to snatch the Catch of the Day and find himself in the "Forthcoming Marriages" section of the Court Circular.'

'I take your point,' said the Dowager Duchess. 'So, by both of you travelling to Switzerland, I raise the chances of both of my unmarried offspring dinging the church bells?'

'You're bong on the nose there, Mater,' said Twinks, rolling on camomile lawns because her mother appeared to have swallowed whole the gubbins she'd just been fed.

Blotto didn't take it up immediately with his sister, but he did feel a little put out by what had been said in the Blue Morning Room. More than put out, even slightly cheated. He knew Twinks would never play him a diddler's hand, but she had led him astray. She'd told him that his excursion to Switzerland would be to enjoy the winter sports. She had told their mother he would be out there on a bride-hunt. Whereas the first suggestion tickled his trews mightily, the second really put lumps in his custard.

'I mean, maybe,' Blotto said to his confidant, 'Twinks has got some plumpilicious planette in her brainbox and everything'll turn up sunny-side, but she could have uncaged the ferrets to me about it beforehand. When she was talking to the Mater, she sounded like they were both tickling the same trout. By Denzil, if the Mater's recruited Twinks into her murdy plots to snap the marital manacles on me, then I may as well hoist up the white flag straight away. But I mean, Twinks would never sell me down the plughole, would she?' he ended on a note of positive pleading.

From inside his stall, the hunter Mephistopheles whinnied assurance that Twinks would never do that.

Still, Blotto didn't feel completely reassured.

And then, of course, he had to apologise to Mephistopheles for the fact that he was going abroad during the hunting season.

2

The Real Reason

When in London overnight, the habitual accommodation for Blotto and Twinks was the Savoy Hotel. But if they were only in Town for the inside of a day, both of them had favoured haunts. For Blotto, it was The Grenadiers, a gentlemen's club know to all its members as 'The Gren'. Here he was guaranteed copious supplies of nursery food, club claret, brandy and circular conversations with his old muffin-toasters from Eton.

Like most clubs, The Gren had many regulations, but the most important one was that, on the premises, nobody should talk about work. Since none of the members did any work, this wasn't hard to comply with.

Twinks's regular watering hole was also a club, but in more gracious and *soigné* style. It was called 'The Lady Graduates' Club', though there was a level of irony in the name. At the time, there were very few Lady Graduates. Though the University of London had granted degrees to women in 1878, Oxford didn't get round to doing so until 1920. And Cambridge still showed no signs of following those pioneering examples.

So, many members of The Lady Graduates' Club were not graduates at all. They were just highly intelligent women who thought they deserved graduate status – and would have had it but for the retrograde educational system of the time. The LGC was one of the few London clubs where prospective candidates had to pass an entrance examination. (Had such a system obtained at The Gren, its membership would have been considerably reduced. And there was no way Blotto would have been allowed in. He had never passed an examination in his life.)

So it was that Twinks, whose dainty toes had never touched the ancestral paving of a university except as a visitor, had no difficulty in joining the club. In fact, she was the only member ever to have scored one hundred per cent in the entrance examination.

The club was a tall Georgian building in Mayfair. Though its décor shared many details with a place like The Gren – panelled walls, dusty portraits and shelves of leather-bound books – there were minor, but significant, differences. For one thing, the leather-bound books were sometimes opened and quite frequently read, something that had never happened at The Gren.

Also, at The Lady Graduates' Club, there were plentiful vases of flowers in evidence. Whereas, at The Gren, even buttonholes were frowned on. A woman's touch . . .

The Lady Graduates' Club regulations banned three topics of conversation. The first was Women's Rights – the members had all assumed from birth that they had the right to do anything they wanted to, so there was no need to talk about them.

The second banned subject was children. Though the members all joined under their maiden names, the list included quite a lot of mothers. But none of them would have been so crass as to mention, within the club's hallowed portals, a baby's first smile, a daughter's balletic skills or the sporting prowess of a son at prep school.

The third anathema was relationships with men. Mooning and mawking about the blatant inadequacies of the masculine gender was so frowned on that the club's main source of alcohol was known as 'The No Sympathy Bar'. There were plenty of other places where women could commiserate and weep over broken hearts. Venues such as hairdresser's, couturier's, powder rooms and tea shops fitted the bill. Such mushy talk was very properly not allowed in The Lady Graduates' Club.

The guardian at the gates of the No Sympathy Bar was a daunting figure, dressed always in black, who was known as Professor Eudoria Haggis. Sadly, her professorship was as fictional as most of the other members' degrees. Though her academic prowess in chemistry exceeded that of most male academics, in the 1920s there seemed to be no prospect of any woman ever being elevated to professorial status. And all her significant – indeed, ground-breaking – advances in the field of chemistry had been claimed as their own by her older male colleagues.

So, never one to mope over missed opportunities, Professor Eudoria Haggis directed her considerable scientific abilities into the invention of new cocktails. With the result that the range offered at the No Sympathy Bar was the most extensive, certainly in London and possibly in the entire world.

Twinks arrived in The Lady Graduates' Club before the person she was meeting, so at once went through to the bar to check out Professor Eudoria Haggis's newest creations.

'My latest,' the barkeeper confided, 'is called the "Suffra-Jet". That's with a "j" rather than a "g", because its impact is like a jet of icy water in the face.' She gave a vigorous judder to her cocktail shaker. 'I was just making one as you arrived, Twinks. As of this moment, the compound has only been tasted by myself under, it goes without saying, laboratory conditions. Would you care to try it?'

'Do the French like cheese?' came the rhetorical response.

Professor Eudoria Haggis removed the top from her shaker and poured out some of the contents. The green glass of tall flute disguised the concoction's colour.

'May I ask what are the put-ins to your potion?' said Twinks.

'You may ask, and I may tell you *some* of them.' Haggis leant pointedly on the word.

'Go on then. Uncage the ferrets.'

'The principal ingredients of a Suffra-Jet,' said the Professor mysteriously, 'are gin, brandy and Sancerre.'

'All plumpilicious,' said Twinks.

'Indeed. And then, of course,' Haggis added slyly, 'there are other components that I would not identify under torture.'

'Larksissimo!' breathed Twinks. 'And might these components have fitted the pigeonhole of a laboratory rather than a liquor store?'

Professor Eudoria Haggis smiled enigmatically, as she pushed the glass towards her customer. 'They might, indeed.'

'Splendissimo,' said Twinks. Everyone at The Lady Graduates' Club knew how much time their barkeeper spent researching her cocktails. Hours of experimentation went into every one, and she only introduced a new

13

creation when she had convinced herself that no further improvement could be made. (Nor did anyone ever ask for precise descriptions of the chemicals used. Better not to know. The legality and safety of the ingredients was never questioned either. The institution's private club status evaded inspections from over-curious government bodies.)

Twinks looked into the glass to find the contents were an almost fluorescent blue, which against the green glass looked strangely alien, a compound from another planet. She took a sip of her first Suffra-Jet.

Twinks had enjoyed cocktails in the past but had never achieved the nirvana described by her brother when he first encountered a St Louis Steamhammer. Blotto, not a man given to verbal embellishment, had waxed almost poetic on the subject. 'It was as if the back of my spoffing head had exploded into fragments of confetti, which had then buzzed around like fumacious fruitflies before settling back into the old brainbox.'

One mouthful of a Suffra-Jet, though, and Twinks knew what her brother had been going on about. The initial sharpness of the taste, the tickle of bubbles against her hard palate, gave way to a tingling sensation which swept languorously through her body till reaching its furthest extremities.

The barometer of Twinks's feelings was set permanently to 'Sunny'. Had there been an 'Extremely Sunny' section, the Suffra-Jet would have pushed the pointer into it.

'Does it pass?' asked Professor Eudoria Haggis anxiously.

'"Does it pass?"' Twinks beamed. 'It passes with colours flying so high that they burst through the troposphere and scrape the edge of the stratosphere! Add it to the club's list of cocktails as quick as a lizard's lick! Professor, with this

14

buzzbanger of a creation you deserve a spoffing award for improving the lot of humankind! The Suffra-Jet is a—'

The encomium might have continued, had Twinks's flow not been interrupted by the arrival of the fellow member she had agreed to meet that morning. Berengaria ffrench-Windeau was an imposingly willowy creature dressed in floor-length grey, who added to her considerable height a peacock feather arising from a jewelled headband. Her dark hair was cut boyishly short and from her crimson lips there always depended an ebony cigarette holder the length of a riding crop. At its end glowed a Turkish cigarette wrapped in pink paper with a gold band at the holder end.

'Twinks daaarling!' she trilled. 'What absolute heaven in a hug to see you!'

'Jollissimo, Berry!' The air around their faces was kissed extravagantly before Twinks went on, 'Don't say the tinjiest word, Berry, till you have tasted the No Sympathy's new sublimity.' Dainty fingernails tapped on the bar. 'Another Suffra-Jet, please, Professor!'

The cocktail provided had exactly the same effect on Berengaria ffrench-Windeau as it had had on Twinks. Into every vein of each woman well-being flowed. After copious compliments to the Suffra-Jet's creator, they took their refills across to a panelled alcove in the No Sympathy Bar.

'So, Berry,' said Twinks, 'your message very definitely kept the hood on the hawk. Why the secrecy? Can you inkle me what it was all about? Come on, uncage the ferrets!'

'Well, Twinks daaarling . . .' Berengaria ffrench-Windeau took a long pull on her cigarette holder. 'The reason I need to talk to you concerns my younger sister.'

'Aurelia!' said Twinks. 'I popped the partridge on that as soon as I got the message. What horracious scrape has the little droplet neckdeeped into this time?'

Twinks knew what she was talking about. Aurelia ffrench-Windeau had quite a track record of misbehaviour. Having seen off a series of governesses, she had been sent, at the age of twelve, to a boarding school so upmarket that all the staff had titles. There her copybook had been blotted so many times that it no longer resembled a copybook.

If there were school rules to be broken, Aurelia ffrench-Windeau would break them. If there were schoolteachers to be cheeked, she would cheek them. If there were cigarettes to be smoked, she would smoke them. If there was alcohol to be drunk, she would drink it. If there were ploughboys from the nearby farms to be consorted with, she would consort with them. If there were illegal London nightclubs to be smuggled away to at weekends, she would be smuggled away to them.

She very quickly became known around staffrooms as the 'Devil of the Dorms'. She was perverse, reckless and uncontrollable.

The only thing any schoolteacher found to commend in Aurelia ffrench-Windeau was her sporting prowess. She was a bit like Blotto in that respect, a natural at all sports. Whatever the size of the ball, the shape of the instrument with which she was hitting it, or the complication of the apparatus required, Aurelia would triumph over any opposition.

Her skill was innate. Like Blotto, she didn't have to practise. Like Blotto, she picked up the skills of any new sport almost instantly. But, of course – as Twinks and any other female of her generation knew – athletic prowess was not so highly regarded in a woman as in a man. Modest ability in a man was lauded. Sporting genius in a woman was ignored. It was regarded as a short-term diversion until she got on to the main purpose of her gender. The production of new twiglets for family trees.

The last news Twinks had had of Aurelia ffrench-Windeau had been of her expulsion from the upmarket school, for finally breaking one rule too many. Rumour had it that her transgression involved actually infiltrating a local ploughboy into her dormitory. So, Twinks waited with interest for Berengaria's update on her sister's most recent misdemeanours.

'Well,' said Berengaria, 'the Mater finally put her foot down.'

Twinks awaited with interest for further details. When the Dowager Duchess of Tawcester put her foot down, the entire planet trembled. But she knew the mother of Berry to be made of flimsier fabric. This was proved by the fact that she hadn't put her foot down earlier to curb her younger daughter's excesses.

'She's decided,' Berengaria went on, 'that Aurelia needs the discipline of a religious order.'

'You're not telling me the little greengage is going to become a spoffing nun? If I ever met anyone less suited to the wearing of a wimple, then I—'

'No, no! The idea of my sister as "a bride of God" . . . I think we'd pretty soon see God in the divorce courts.'

'Aurelia's never going to be an "GLG", is she?' said Twinks.

Berengaria chuckled. 'No, she is not.' 'GLG' was an acronym of the slang kind so beloved by the aristocracy. It stood for 'Good Little Girl' and was almost always used in a cynical or pejorative way.

There was nothing that would have offended Aurelia more than being described as a 'GLG'.

'So, what are you cluntering on about, Berry?' asked Twinks.

'The Mater thinks that the sibling might behave better – or at least be less embarrassing to the family – if she left the Land of the Golden Lions for a whilette.'

'What, you mean the poor little shrimplet should go *abroad*?' Twinks wasn't quite as appalled by the idea of leaving England as her brother, but still thought of it as a big step.

'Yes. The Mater decreed that Aurelia should go to Switzerland. To a school run by nuns.'

'A *finishing* school?' suggested Twinks.

'You're bong on the nose there,' said Berry.

'In the hope that it would put a *finish* to her fumacious behaviour?'

'Give that pony a rosette!' said Berry.

'And is the planette working out, ticking the tick-box?' asked Twinks.

'Well, that's what's putting lumps in the Mater's custard.'

'Oh?'

'The fact is, Twinks, that we don't know. We haven't heard a plip from the little droplet since she arrived out there.'

'And is she normally regular on the letter-lobbing front?'

'No, she's hopeless.'

'Then why are you donning your worry-boots?'

'Because the Mater wasn't expecting anything from Aurelia herself. But she had contacted the school for an update and hasn't heard a squiffin.'

'She wrote to them?'

18

'Yes, piles of letters. Even a couple of telegrams.'

'Addressed to whom?'

'The Mother Superior. She runs the place. Sister Anneliese-Marie.'

'And got nothing back?'

'No. My view is that Aurelia's probably somehow heading the letters off, bribing the postman not to deliver them, but the Mater's not convinced. She does tend to overdramatise things. Her latest worry is that there's been an avalanche and the whole finishing school has been swept off the mountainside.'

'So, you're saying, Berry, that someone should turn their truffler on to this problemette?'

'You've popped the partridge there, Twinks. And I know it's something I should really be doing myself. And I would, but I can't . . . because of . . . because of . . .'

Berengaria's hands seemed to be gesturing to their surroundings. It took a moment before Twinks, usually so acute, caught on to her meaning. Two years previously, her friend had rather let the side down by getting married. And she was now the mother of a demanding one-year-old. But, of course, such a thing could not be mentioned within the hallowed portals of The Lady Graduates' Club.

'I read your semaphore, Berry,' said Twinks. 'You're asking me if I would go out to Switzerland and find out what's happened to your sister?'

'If you'd consider it . . . What do you think of the idea?'

There was a glow of excitement in her azure eyes as Twinks murmured, 'Jollissimo!'

Then they went back to the bar and ordered two more Suffra-Jets.

3

Off in the Lagonda!

It went without saying that three of them set off in the Lagonda from Tawcester Towers. The aristocratic siblings would no more embark on a foreign adventure without their chauffeur Corky Froggett than Twinks would leave behind her sequined reticule or Blotto his cricket bat. And Corky would have been seriously miffed if they hadn't included him.

As a man, Corky Froggett had come into his own during what he referred to as 'the recent little dust-up in France'. He was a finely tuned killing machine, never happier than facing the enemy from behind an Accrington-Murphy machine gun. He deeply regretted the Armistice of 11 November 1918 which put an end to his harmless pleasures, and knew that civilian life thereafter was bound to be an anti-climax.

But, not being by nature one to brood, Corky Froggett had made the best of a bad job and returned to his chauffeuring duties at Tawcester Towers. He ensured that no mote of dust was allowed to remain on the Lagonda's immaculate dark blue bodywork for more than a nanosecond. And devoted the rest of his considerable energies to looking after the needs of his young master, Devereux Lyminster, and the young mistress, Lady Honoria. His long-term ambition was to lay down his life in the defence of one or both of them. So far, this aspiration had not been realised, but he lived in hope.

Summer was really the best season for driving the Lagonda. Blotto knew of few things, away from the hunting field, which were more exhilarating than rocketing down the middle of the narrow lanes of Tawcestershire, the wind rippling through his wheat-coloured hair, his hands on the steering wheel of his magnificent monster. There were parallels with the hunting field, too. As Blotto and Mephistopheles led the rest of the hunt in full cry, they wrought untold destruction on the fences and fields of the local farmers. In the same way, the Lagonda wrought untold destruction on anything that stood in its way. In its wake, the roadside ditches were full of displaced ox-carts, pony traps and vicars knocked off bicycles.

Blotto relished the prospect of creating similar mayhem across Europe. But, of course, it was the wrong time of year. He wouldn't be able to have the wind rippling through his wheat-coloured hair. For the current excursion, the Lagonda's roof would have to be closed all the time. Twinks regretted this because it would limit her view of the beautiful continental scenery. Blotto and Corky Froggett were unmoved. They never noticed scenery and, anyway, were both of the opinion that the best views in the known universe were to be found on the Tawcester Towers estate.

Needless to say, Twinks would be the navigator. Corky Froggett was a great student of maps who put in some homework before setting off to an unfamiliar destination, but Twinks was more skilled. As for Blotto, his approach was more hit and miss. Faced with a choice at a junction, he would take the road that looked more interesting, convinced that he'd somehow end up where he wanted to get to. Past experience had revealed this system not to be infallible.

Fortunately, though he knew his way around the roads and lanes of Tawcestershire, on longer excursions he almost always had his sister by his side, giving him due warning of the next turning or road hazard he was about to encounter. She was also good at timing journeys and estimating likely arrival times at the various stops along the way.

'Beezer wheeze,' he once said to her, 'you having all this gin-gen at the end of your dainties. Means, when you tell me which direction to pongle off in, I can drive without thinking.'

Twinks was far too loyal to point out that her brother did everything without thinking.

'It's not much of a burden on the brainbox,' she said. 'Just a matter of memorising maps. A machine could do it.'

Blotto had roared with laughter at this. 'Oh yes? And I'm an Apache dancer. A spoffing machine that tells you which way to drive? Well, that's about as likely as a boddo without a topper being allowed into Ascot!'

'It may happen, Blotto me old tin of dubbin. We live in an age of amazing inventions. Fifty years ago, there was no spoffing electricity.'

'No, Twinks me old cheese-melter,' he agreed, 'but I think it'll be a long time before electricity replaces you as a Lag-navigator. Don't you agree, Corky?' he had shouted to the back of the car.

'I certainly do, milord. Electricity's not natural,' the chauffeur said darkly. He hadn't grown up in a house where electricity featured. And he was properly suspicious of things he hadn't grown up with. Most new inventions, he knew, were tempting providence. It'd end in tears. Electricity was a good example. What would happen if the wires got punctured and electricity started spilling all over the floor? Then people'd be sorry.

As the siblings set out on their journey, there were no fond farewells from their mother. But then there was never any fond anything from the Dowager Duchess. Her only concern in this particular instance was that Blotto and Twinks should not return till after Christmas.

And, as for Loofah, it would never have occurred to either of them to say goodbye to him. Loofah wouldn't notice their absence from Tawcester Towers. He didn't notice much, actually.

They set off relatively early ... well, as soon as Blotto had demolished the last morsel of bacon, sausage, eggs, kipper, devilled kidney and kedgeree in his customary gargantuan breakfast. Their luggage was secured in the Lagonda's dickey. Blotto had double-checked that his cricket bat was safely stowed on board. Twinks had checked the contents of her sequined reticule, the depository for all her travelling essentials. Because you never knew when such things might become necessary, she had included some self-igniting fireworks.

Corky had assembled the more practical equipment. One of the few things he knew about Switzerland was that a lot of snow and ice featured there. So, he filled the car's secret under-chassis compartments with shovels, pickaxes, chains and blankets. Corky Froggett was not a man to be outdone by such trifles as the weather.

Blotto drove, with Twinks beside him and the chauffeur on the back seat. As ever, the Lagonda surged along the crest of the road, leaving its customary human detritus in the ditches to either side. According to Twinks's plans, they reached Dover in time for the five o'clock afternoon ferry and were checked into the hotel she had booked in Calais in time to enjoy a lavish dinner.

A reluctant Corky Froggett was persuaded to eat with them. 'The French are less formal about social division than we are in the Land of the Golden Lions,' Twinks reassured him. 'Because of that fumacious Revolution they had. Their aristocracy didn't amount to a ladle of cockleshells before that. Now they haven't even got an aristocracy.'

Blotto magnanimously agreed. 'So, it'll all be creamy éclair for you to share the nosebags with us, Corky . . . even though you are, by the length of a transatlantic cable, so much our social inferior.'

'Thank you very much, milord,' said a humble but gratified chauffeur.

Though Twinks had a more cosmopolitan palate, Blotto and Corky did not endear themselves to the hotel management by refusing to touch any food that had a vestige of a sauce on it.

Their journey to Switzerland was uneventful. Needless to say, Twinks's carefully planned itinerary worked perfectly. The Lagonda arrived at the various gorging and gulping stops within seconds of her predicted times. And landed up on cue at the Swiss border.

Blotto was a little miffed that they had to get out of the car to have their passports checked. He felt the eminence of the Lyminster family should have allowed them through on a nod. Foreigners, he knew, though, could be very small-minded.

Standing for the first time on Swiss soil, Twinks arranged an elegant grey cashmere wrap around her delicate shoulders and breathed in deeply through her dainty nostrils. 'Splendissimo, isn't it, Blotto me old sardine-tin-opener?'

'What's splendissimo?' he asked.

'The air.'

'Air?' He took a deep breath but was less overwhelmed by the experience than his sister. 'Well, it's . . . air,' he said.

Corky Froggett was also breathing deeply, though for reasons that had nothing to do with the air quality. He was hoping that travelling through Switzerland would have less adverse impact on him than travelling through France had. All his memories of the latter country were tied up with 'the recent little dust-up in France'. Being on French soil – and not being behind an Accrington-Murphy machine gun with a licence to kill people – had been a profound emotional wrench for him.

Passport formalities concluded, the three in the Lagonda set off for their ultimate destination.

The little village of Luzvimmen was perched on an impossibly picturesque mountainside. The mountain itself was called the Altzberg. Though Luzvimmen had not been in the vanguard of developing its winter sports business, it was quickly catching up with the more advanced resorts like St Moritz, Gstaad and Davos. A skiing club had been founded in 1910 and soon started to attract upper-class British tourists to its natural sporting facilities. Chalets were converted into hotels and new ones built to accommodate the rising number of guests. The hospitality industry boomed. Pistes were identified and defined. Locals honed their skills as ski instructors. Luzvimmen had not yet got any of the new-fangled ski lifts which were being developed, but it was only a matter of time.

The village also boasted a convenient lake, ideal for skating, and gentle slopes for children on sledges. But perhaps the feature that made it most famous – and would make it even more famous in time to come – was its extraordinarily dangerous racing toboggan track known as the Croissant Run. The notoriety of this – and an impressive list of fatalities – made it an irresistible attraction to a certain kind of young man with too much bone in their skulls to have any room left for brain. In other words, the kind of people who had been Blotto's social circle all his life.

In the foothills of the Altzberg, as the Lagonda started its long haul up the icy incline, Twinks noticed a series of large yellow warehouses, which looked more like military installations than anything else. From the signs reading 'Chäs Luzvimmen' on them, she deduced that they were connected with the local cheesemaking industry.

Blotto didn't deduce anything. Deduction wasn't his strong suit. (Actually, his only really strong suit was the tweed one he was wearing that day. As was common among people of his class, the garment had been worn by his father, the late Duke of Lyminster. Clothes, like furniture – and indeed money – should ideally be inherited. Only parvenus and solicitors coveted new stuff.)

As the party in the Lagonda approached, they saw that, above and below the main village, stood two surprisingly large buildings. The one lower down the mountainside, built in solid stone, might have been turned into an hotel like so many other Luzvimmen properties, but for the fact that it was owned by the Church. It was a convent, run by a minor order of Roman Catholic nuns. And, like many convents, it was also a school. It was, in fact, the finishing school in which Aurelia ffrench-Windeau had been enrolled.

The other large building, higher up above the village, was a castle (or 'Schloss') called, with remarkable lack of originality, Schloss Luzvimmen. It was one of those structures which promotes amazement, not only because of its dominating position, but also because its construction must have been so difficult. How, with the limited techno- logy of the Middle Ages, could men have transported so much stone up to a craggy promontory which, for most of the year, was buried under thick snow? It was a question which would continue to be asked for many years to come. And no one would ever be able to provide a satisfactory answer.

Blotto's opinion, when he first saw the Schloss Luzvimmen, was that it wasn't a real castle. He seen a few schlosses and even more chateaux on his travels and he could never understand why Europeans always got it wrong. Towers should have flat tops, like they did in the Land of the Golden Lions, but foreigners always put spoffing pointed hats on top of them.

'Not to shimmy round the shrubbery, Twinks,' he often complained to her, 'a tower shouldn't look like a fumacious upturned pencil. For a castle to be rightfully given the name-tag of "castle", the top of its walls should be granulated.'

'Crenellated,' Twinks always said softly.

* * *

The hotel into which Twinks had booked the English party (called, with remarkable lack of originality, Hotel Luzvimmen) was a conversion rather than a new build. Its original owner must have been a person of considerable wealth. Though constructed in chalet style with low sloping gabled roofs, overhanging eaves and balconies, it didn't conform to the usual modest chalet dimensions. It was huge, and the interior had been decorated to the highest specification, making it a surprisingly luxurious hotel for a small village like Luzvimmen. Twinks recognised the hand of some canny entrepreneur preparing to capitalise on the growing popularity of winter sports.

Blotto, as usual, didn't recognise anything.

Assiduous hotel staff had rushed out on the arrival of the Lagonda. Having taken Blotto and Twinks's luggage from the dickey, they directed Corky Froggett to the garages round the back. (He, of course, given his lowly status as a chauffeur, was not going to be billeted in the main hotel. A room in a modest nearby *pension* had been booked for him.)

The more Twinks looked around the hotel foyer, the more familiar elements of it became. Bizarrely, they reminded her of the entrance hall at Tawcester Towers. Partly, it was the stags' heads and other hunting trophies on the walls, but there was also something about the colour scheme that struck a chord.

It came back to her. These were exactly the same colours that had been used in the short-lived makeover of Tawcester Towers by a dubious, corrupt company called Aristotours.

So, she was prepared to recognise the voice that welcomed them into Hotel Luzvimmen.

'Lady Honoria! Lord Devereux! What a surprise to find you in Switzerland!'

She turned from her scrutiny of the décor to see, standing behind the reception desk, the former Master of the Revels at Tawcester Towers, and total crook, Ulrich Weissfeder.

4

The Finishing School

Even if she hadn't been aware of Ulrich Weissfeder's track record, his greeting would still have sparked Twinks's suspicions. Her letter to make the booking at Hotel Luzvimmen had been written on Tawcester Towers headed notepaper. For the hotel manager to describe their arrival as a surprise was, at the very least, bizarre.

But, though he had called them by name, Ulrich Weissfeder appeared to be in no hurry to remember their previous encounter.

Twinks greeted him as 'Herr Weissfeder', thus acknowledging that they had met before but without expanding on the circumstances. In her mind, his card was marked, though. If any skulduggery was unearthed during their stay in Luzvimmen, it was more than likely that Ulrich Weissfeder would be involved in it.

The morning after their arrival at the hotel, Twinks was determined to get started on her mission: discovering the whereabouts of Aurelia ffrench-Windeau. And that would involve a visit to the finishing school in which the young lady was enrolled, the building they had seen as they approached the village. She had the address – she knew it was called the Convent of the Sacred Icicle – and a very helpful girl on the hotel reception gave her directions. Twinks spoke such good Swiss German – and equally good Swiss French and Swiss Italian, had they been required – that, if her details hadn't been registered, it would never have occurred to the receptionist that she might be English.

It was recommended that she should book one of the hotel's horse-drawn sleighs for the short journey. This she did. Travelling around the narrow village streets in the Lagonda was evidently not going to be practical.

Before she set out, Twinks breakfasted with her brother in the hotel's dining room, which commanded unfeasibly beautiful views over the Alpine snowscape. She commented approvingly on the vista. Blotto, less susceptible to the allure of the natural world outside Tawcester Towers, complained that 'It's all spoffing white.'

Though the breakfast menu did not feature the same delicacies as would have graced the chafing dishes at Tawcester Towers, the range was extensive. The siblings filled up royally on bread, pastries, eggs, ham and salami-style sausage. Blotto, however, was confused by some of the items on display. He had to ask his sister to identity a glutinous white substance as yoghurt. He then wanted to know:

How it was made, and

That being the case, why anyone would want to eat the fumacious stuff?

He then entered into an ultimately unrewarding conversation with one of the waitresses as he tried to explain to her what a kipper was. Clearly, they didn't have them in Switzerland, which only went to show what a peculiar country he had landed in.

'And, if that didn't take Queen Victoria's biscuit,' he confided to his sister, 'the boddoes here can't even make proper cheese.' 'Proper cheese', in Blotto's view, was called Cheddar and came in slabs with the consistency of soap (and, sometimes, the flavour too). He pointed to the offending slices on the breakfast table. 'That looks like the murdy moths have been at it. The globbins is full of horracious holes.'

Twinks, of course, knew why there were holes in Swiss cheese. (She did know everything, after all.) She was aware of the two most popular theories explaining the phenomenon. First, that bacteria in the starter used gave off carbon dioxide which formed bubbles in the mixture. And, second, that the holes grew around hay particulates from the buckets in which the cheese making milk had been stored. Having considered the scientific evidence (something she always did in such circumstances), Twinks was an advocate of the hay theory.

But she knew, from long experience, that some things just weren't worth the bother of explaining to her brother, so she made no comment.

After they'd finished breakfast, Blotto was keen to know his sister's plans for the day and was not too disappointed to be informed that his gender would exclude him from joining in her visit to a convent. He reconciled himself to being left to his own devices ... 'though what a boddo does in a spoffing icehouse like this, I haven't a mouse-squeak of an idea.'

Twinks had planned her wardrobe for the Swiss climate and, swathed in white fur like an exotic snowman, set off

32

in the horse-drawn sleigh with a liveried driver, for the Convent of the Sacred Icicle.

It was a stone building of considerable antiquity, some twenty minutes down the mountainside from Luzvimmen. Twinks was lulled by the scenic beauty, the clop of the horse's hooves and the swish of the metal runners on the ice-hard roadway. She didn't exactly doze, but still came to with a jolt as the sleigh stopped outside the convent's massive wooden doors.

The liveried driver, assuming she was a native of the country, told her in German Swiss that, though he would normally escort her and knock on the door, it was not proper for him to do so at an all-female institution.

She estimated that her visit would take less than an hour and the liveried driver said he would wait for her. Presumably, given the job he did, he was reconciled to spending much of his time waiting in icy conditions. He certainly did not appear to be put out at the prospect.

Twinks, noting with gratitude that the front path had been cleared of snow and gritted, pulled at the long chain, which set booming reverberations of a bell echoing from inside. The doors were opened by a young novice, whose unwillingness to speak made Twinks wonder whether she'd taken a vow of silence.

'My name is Lady Honoria Lyminster,' she announced, again in fluent Swiss German. 'And I wish to see the Mother Superior.'

Still, the girl showed no inclination to talk.

'I wrote to her. She is expecting me.' This wasn't strictly true. In fact, it was totally untrue. Twinks had considered writing to the convent but rejected the idea because it gave the Mother Superior the option of refusing her request for an interview. The surprise value of turning up unannounced might, Twinks had decided, work in her favour.

Her assertiveness (born of the Lyminster family's many generations' experience of bullying serfs and villeins) did indeed work a treat. The subdued novice, remaining silent, ushered the visitor inside and closed the doors behind her. Twinks found herself in an austere stone hallway, whose walls were completely unadorned and lit by tall candles in torchières. The girl led the way along a similarly featureless passage. Somewhere in the interior unison female voices were singing musical scales.

Their progress was halted by the appearance, from a corridor that cut across the hallway, of a small procession. There was a nun at the front and the back and between them walked a line of girls, probably aged around sixteen. Their uniform of black skirts and stiff white blouses echoed the monochrome of the sisters' habits. The girls were only distinguished from each other by the colour of their uncovered hair – Mediterranean black, Scandinavian blonde, lots of English mouse, and a few redheads (those Vikings got everywhere). Though silent and outwardly obedient, the expression on their faces suggested that some had thoughts which might not match the purity of their surroundings.

None of the girls was the missing Aurelia ffrench-Windeau.

After the finishing school pupils had passed, the novice led the way to a tall metal-studded door, outside which she paused. For the first time she spoke. 'I will check,' she said in breathy Swiss German. 'The Reverend Mother may be at her devotions. At such times she cannot be interrupted.'

Twinks decided not to take issue at that point. If she was denied access to the Mother Superior, though, a high horse might have to be mounted. And few had superior equestrian skills on a high horse than Lady Honoria Lyminster.

The girl tapped on the door and was granted admission. With a gesture telling the visitor to wait, she disappeared inside. Twinks gave them two minutes, checked by the pocket watch in her sequined reticule, and then, taking affairs into her own hands, stormed into the inner sanctum.

A woman of extremely broad mind, she still could not imagine how any definition of the word 'devotions' could encompass the actions that she found the Mother Superior performing in her office.

The woman, from the neck upwards, was dressed like a nun, wimple and all. Lower down, though, things were different. She wore a white basque, white ankle-length bloomers with lacy details and, surprisingly, black leather workman's boots. Her feet were placed on two wooden boards supported some six inches above the floor by small wheels. She kept shifting from side to side, the strength in her thighs controlling the boards and preventing them from slipping away underneath her feet. Moving forward and back in rhythm, she balanced their motion and achieved a stasis that could only have come with long practice.

'What,' asked Twinks, 'in the name of Wilberforce, are you spoffing well doing?'

This enquiry was met by a fierce 'Ssh!' from the Mother Superior.

'She is not to be disturbed,' said the novice shyly, 'during her devotions.'

Twinks was so surprised that she kept silent. If she

35

actually hoped to get information out of the woman, she would probably be in with a better chance if she bided her time. There were two wooden chairs either side of the large desk. Twinks sat in one of them to wait, puzzling over the nature of the devotions and the identity of the deity to whom they were being addressed.

There was perhaps a clue in the way the Mother Superior ended her ritual. Straightening her legs, so that the two wheeled boards came together forming a single flat surface, she stood totally still for a full minute. Then, with the words, 'Praise be to God,' she hopped off the platform, reached to pick her black robes off the desk, pulled them over her head and subsided into the vacant chair.

Now representing the archetype of a black-clad Mother Superior, she inclined graciously towards her visitor, smiled a serene smile, and said, in perfect English, 'Good morning. How may I be of assistance to you?'

Instinctively, Twinks recognised that she was up against a woman of strong character, possibly even of a strength of character approaching her own. 'How did you know,' she asked in perfect Swiss German, 'that I am English?'

'If you think there are any secrets in Luzvimmen,' the nun replied, 'then you have never lived in a small village.'

Twinks, of course, never had lived in a small village. She had always lived in a large castle with a family which owned a lot of small villages. But she didn't think it was the moment to mention this. Instead, she asked, 'So you got a twingle of my arrival from Ulrich Weissfeder at the hotel, did you?'

'From him among others.'

Their conversation continued with each using the other's language. This was an expression of some kind of competitive spark between them.

36

'Anyway, what should I call you?' the Mother Superior went on. 'Lady Honoria?'

'Everyone calls me "Twinks".'

'Then I will call you "Twinks".'

'And what should I call you? "Mother Superior"?'

'No. Call me "Sam".'

'"Sam"?' Twinks was astonished. 'Why, in the name of ginger?'

'When I entered the order, I was given the name of "Sister Anneliese-Marie". The initials spell out "Sam".'

'Tickey-tockey,' said Twinks. '"Sam" it is.' Convenient, she thought, that 'Sister' and 'Schwester' both began with the same letter, so the nickname worked in both languages.

'Anyway, Twinks . . .' The Mother Superior leant forward over her desk, 'what has brought you all the way from Tawcester Towers to Luzvimmen?'

Resisting the instinct to question how her home address was known, Twinks cut straight to the truth. 'I have a chumbo called Berengaria ffrench-Windeau, who's got a droplet of a sister called Aurelia. Aurelia was exported out here to your finishing school and Berry hasn't heard a mouse-squeak from the poor little thimble for yonks and yonklets. So, I've pongled out here to check whether any part of the Stilton is iffy.'

The names had their effect on the Mother Superior. The moment her visitor had finished speaking, she directed towards the novice a nod which sent her scuttling out of the room at once.

'You must understand, Twinks,' she said when the door had closed, 'that you are inside a religious institution . . . on hallowed ground, if you like. And some mysteries are encompassed by the Almighty Mystery that is God.'

Twinks was not awed by the reference. 'If, Sam, you think you can use God as an excuse to sell me down the river for a handful of winkle shells, then you have under-estimated the adversary you are up against.'

'Please do not talk of "adversaries". We are in a place of peace. And I am a woman of peace.'

'Oh yes?' said Twinks. 'And I'm an Apache dancer.'

'Am I to gather, Twinks, that you are a woman without religion?'

'Not by the longest chalk stream in the kingdom!' She was appalled by the suggestion. 'I have as much spoffing religion as anyone else in England! I always write "Church of England" when I'm filling in fumacious forms. I go to the Tawcester Towers chapel regularly every Easter and Christmas to chant out the Godtwaddle. And I believe what it is convenient for me to believe. The Church of England is unlike Roman Catholicism. We're not constantly being told what our faith should incorporate. Such decisions are left to the whimsy of the individual. A boddo can believe as much or as little as a boddo wishes to believe.'

After this eloquent – and possibly over-enthusiastic – exposition of her national religion, Twinks pressed on. 'Aurelia ffrench-Windeau . . . are you saying the poor little greengage never pongled out here to be finished? That she never reached first base?'

'I am not saying that, Twinks. The information you received from her sister Berengaria is indeed correct. Aurelia did arrive here some months ago, and was enrolled in the finishing school which I run here in the Convent of the Sacred Icicle.'

'Larksissimo!' said Twinks. 'Well, is she finished yet? Done to a turn, eh? I would like to see the little thimble.'

'I'm afraid that is impossible.'

'What do you mean – impossible? Is the flapperette being held here against her will? Or has she escaped from durance vile and is out in the wicked world?'

'I do not like your choice of expression.' All haughty Mother Superior now. 'No one is held in the Convent of the Sacred Icicle against their will. But some people find here things that they are not expecting.'

'And what does that mean when it's got its spats on?' demanded Twinks.

Sam's mouth took on a pious rigidity. 'It may be hard,' she began, 'to explain this to someone who has no religion.'

'Of course I've got a spoffing religion!' Twinks remonstrated. 'Church of England. I've just told you all about it. Do I have to put on the same cylinder again?'

'No, you don't. All I am saying is that someone with such an unusual approach to religion may not be—'

'What do you mean – unusual approach? It's the English approach. And, if you had had the good fortune to be spawned in the Land of the Golden Lions, you'd know that nothing that happens in England is unusual. It's foreign boddoes who always get things wrong.'

Patiently, the Mother Superior continued with her explanation. 'The fact is that within the Convent of the Sacred Icicle – and the finishing school contained herein – I have witnessed many miracles.'

In response to something she saw in her visitor's expression, she said, 'Yes, and I know the only miracle in the Church of England is that bishops are allowed seats in the House of Lords. But in the Catholic Church, miracles are an important part of our faith. And one of the miracles I have witnessed, not many times but enough to be significant, is the miracle of a young girl finding her vocation, the call from God for her to devote the rest of her life to Him, to become a Bride of Christ.'

'Great whiffling water rats!' said Twinks 'You're not about to tell me that Aurelia ffrench-Windeau has discovered a vocation? That she wants to become a spoffing Bride of Christ? Because, from what her sister Berengaria told me, the little droplet has always been a terror-scamp of the first order. Known at school as the "Devil of the Dorms". If she ever had a vocation, it would be to join Satan's Specials.'

'People can change,' said Sam. 'Particularly girls between the ages of ten and twenty. Here at the Convent of the Sacred Icicle, I have witnessed troublemakers of the most extreme kind seeing the Divine Light and devoting their lives to the Almighty. But I have seen few transformations so complete as that of Aurelia ffrench-Windeau.'

'You're jiggling my kneecap,' said a disbelieving Twinks.

'I am certainly not. Other girls, like the one who admitted you to the convent, have become novices. But Aurelia has that rare vocation which qualifies her to train as an ordinand for the secret order within the order.'

'And what is that, in the name of snitchrags?'

'I told you – it's a secret. And if I told you about it, it would no longer be a secret, would it?'

'I don't believe there is such an order,' said Twinks defiantly. 'And if such a thing did exist, Aurelia joining it is about as likely as finding a trouser press inside this convent. I think you're talking complete globbins.'

'You may think what you wish,' said the Mother Superior severely. 'The fact remains that Aurelia ffrench-Windeau is here in this convent under strict training to join the secret order whose name I cannot speak. That is

40

the reason why she has chosen to cut herself off from all outside influences, including contact with her family back in England. And that is why, Twinks, there is no possibility of your meeting up with the young woman. She is engaged to become a Bride of Christ!'

It was clear that nothing more would be forthcoming from Sister Anneliese-Marie. Twinks reconciled herself to ending the encounter.

But, like any shrewd general, she withdrew from the field of battle with a view to fighting again. The important admission she had obtained from the Mother Superior was that Aurelia was actually inside the convent building.

All she had to do now was to engineer an encounter with the girl. And that was soluble. For someone with a brain the size of Twinks's, all problems were soluble.

There was no novice outside the office door to see her out. Twinks's first thought was to start her search for Aurelia straight away. She moved silently back to the entrance hall to get her bearings about the convent's layout. There were many doors, some of which would undoubtedly be locked.

But she was prevented from extracting the picklocks she always kept in her sequined reticule by the manifestation in front of her of a very short nun. On closer inspection, the shortness was caused by the fact that the woman was bent over with age. The ancient face was sucked in on itself and Twinks had seen fewer wrinkles on a prune. From the nun's belt hung a substantial ring of heavy keys.

'You are the woman from England who is staying at the Hotel Luzvimmen,' the old voice creaked in Swiss German. 'And I know that you understand my language perfectly.'

'You seem to know everything under the umbrella about

me,' said Twinks. 'Might you give me a bit of the old gin-gen about yourself?'

'My name,' said the crone, 'is Sister Benedicta. I started as a novice in the Convent of the Sacred Icicle early in the last century. I am the oldest surviving nun. I am also the one who knows all the history of the order.'

'And do you also know the history of the "secret order within the order"?'

'I know all the secrets,' said the nun confidently.

'And what, in the name of Wilberforce, might persuade you to share those secrets?'

'Nothing!' came the defiant response. 'Otherwise, they wouldn't be secrets, would they?'

The same logic had been used by the Mother Superior. And in both cases it was unarguable. And rather annoying.

Sister Benedicta went on, 'There is, however, a secret within the Convent of the Sacred Icicle which I am prepared to share with you.'

'What is it?'

'Follow me.' Instinctively finding the relevant key from the ring on her belt, the old nun led Twinks through another metal-studded door into a narrow passage lit by flickering torches in sconces. These were spaced far enough apart for their illumination to be totally inadequate. Twinks followed blindly.

The ancient sister's voice was like a rusty door-hinge as she said, 'This place is called "The Convent of the Sacred Icicle" for a reason. Ice is part of its history. It is dedicated to the memory of Saint Liselotte. She was a lonely goatherd, whose beauty made her a magnet of desire for all men, including the wicked Count who lived in Schloss Luzvimmen. A devout Catholic girl, Liselotte said she would rather die than succumb to his advances.

42

'And so she did die. She was stabbed to death by the wicked Count. And do you know what the weapon he used was?'

If Sister Benedicta had been hoping to stage a shock revelation, she was due for a disappointment. Twinks was way ahead of her (as she usually was of most people). 'It was an icicle.'

She continued, because she was (of course) also up to speed on all the clichés of the nascent genre of detective fiction, 'And yes, yes, yes, it melted after Saint Liselotte got coffinated, leaving no traces, so the running sore of a Count never got jumped on by the gendarmerie. He escaped scot-free.'

'All right, that is what happened,' the wizened sister conceded grudgingly. She was quickly elated again, though, as she announced, 'What I am about to show you is, however, one of the most astonishing phenomena in ice that you will ever see!'

They had reached a pair of tall doors, big enough to allow a coach and horses through. This, too, was locked but, once again, Sister Benedicta knew exactly which key was required to open it. With a flourish – and surprising vigour, given her ageing body – she flung the two doors back.

The sight that greeted Twinks was bizarre and shocking. What faced her was a wall of ice, open at the top to daylight. Sun sparkled off the glassy surface and it took her eyes a few moments to adjust to the brightness.

Then she saw that, within the glacier she faced, were suspended two human forms. Men who, presumably, had been frozen in place perhaps centuries before. The opacity of the ice made it impossible to see details of their clothes and faces. They were just threatening outlines, ghostly, dangerous.

Twinks could not stop herself from saying, in shocked tones, 'Great spangled spiders! What, in the name of Viscount Melbourne, are they?'

'What indeed?' said Sister Benedicta. 'They are the protectors of the Convent of the Sacred Icicle – and of the whole of Luzvimmen.'

'How long have they been on ice?' asked Twinks.

'Many years. People say they were frozen there at the time of Wilhelm Tell, the one who will return one day to save Switzerland. Those figures have been there since the foundations of our order, and they, along with Wilhelm Tell, will save us if ever dangers threaten.'

'And what are they called when they've got their spats on?'

'They are known within the convent as "The Phantom Avengers". Sometimes "The Phantom Skiers". They are locked in the ice, awaiting the Last Trump, when they will be freed from their icy prison and find their deserved places at the right hand of God. So the prophecies say.

'But . . .' Through the wrinkles that surrounded them, Sister Benedicta's piercing eyes transfixed the visitor '. . . in the event of there being an earlier threat, the prophecies also say that The Two Avengers will come back to life and emerge from the ice to save the sanctity of this institution and all the inhabitants of Luzvimmen.

'Then, with exemplary brutality, they will wreak their revenge on anyone who threatens to unearth the secrets of the Convent of the Sacred Icicle!'

Twinks was left in no doubt that she was being threatened.

5

Meeting Muffin-Toasters

Going to the right school, if of course you're English (and are there actually any 'right schools' in other countries?), does bestow many advantages. And, on his first day in Luzvimmen, Blotto was once again made aware of that happy situation.

As was frequently the case, without Twinks around he felt at something of a loose end. Still in a slight state of shock at being in a country where people ate yoghurt, had cheese with holes in it and didn't know what a kipper was, he went out onto one of the hotel's many balconies to check whether there was anything interesting to see outside. He was not optimistic. Everything would be covered with snow, and he had never found snow even mildly interesting.

But what Blotto did see, actually on the balcony, was a sight to gladden his heart – stretched out on a lounging chair, one of his old muffin-toasters from Eton. Mutual recognition led instantly into a ritual greeting.

'Ratteley-Baa-Baa!' said Blotto.

45

'Ratteley-Boo-Boo!' his old school-mate responded instinctively.

'How're you pongling, me old fruit-bat?' asked Blotto.

'Knobby as a chest of drawers. And are your suspenders tight, me old shrimping net?'

'Tight as a hippo's hawser, me old boot blackener.'

'Ra-ra!'

'Ra-ra-ra!' Blotto concluded.

These pleasantries over, he took a look at his old friend. Buffy 'Crocker' Wilmslow. Exact contemporaries at Eton. Matching emptinesses within their crania. Both despaired of by the beaks. Both brilliant at cricket, though Blotto was the more successful, if only because of his friend's tendency to get injured.

That was it, you see, the reason why Buffy Wilmslow was nicknamed 'Crocker'. Because he was always getting crocked up. And a transplantation to Switzerland didn't seem to have improved his luck in that respect. There were crutches at the side of his chair and his left leg was encased in plaster.

'Rats in a sandwich, Crocker!' said Blotto. 'Nobbled your knee again, have you?'

'Not the spoffing knee this time, Blotters. Compound fracture of the fibula.'

'How did that carpet unroll? Purler on the pack ice?'

'No. Don't know, Blotto me old running-spike-remover, whether you've heard of a jammy little toboggan test known as the Croissant Run? Tinkle any cowbells?'

'No,' replied Blotto with his customary honesty.

'Well, fact is, Blotto me old curry comb, that the Luzvimmen Croissant Run is absolutely the panda's panties. No boddo who fancies a challenge – particularly one in which he's likely to get coffinated – should pass up the opp of having a wallop at it.'

Blotto's interest was immediately engaged. He was always up for anything that offered the opp of being coffinated. 'So, what, in the name of Gladstone, does a boddo have to do? What, when it's got its spats on, is the Croissant Run?'

'It's total creamy éclair,' Crocker replied. 'The aim of the whole clangdumble is to start at the top and end up at the bottom.'

'Doesn't sound too gummy. Going downhill is as easy as a one-bush maze.' A recollection of something one of the beaks at Eton had tried to teach him worked its way through the fogs of Blotto's brain. 'According to the principle established by Sir Fig Newton, which is known as gravy.'

'Gravity?' Crocker Wilmslow suggested diffidently.

'Tickey-tockey, that's the Johnny!' said Blotto. 'Gravity! Sir Fig Newton sat under a tree, an apple dropped on him, and he also invented cider.'

Buffy Wilmslow, impressed by the breadth of his friend's knowledge, said nothing.

'So, give me, Crocker me old tin of Brasso,' Blotto went on, 'a bit more gin-gen on this Croissant Run. Does a boddo ski down it or skate down it or what?'

'No, no, it's a 'boggan run. Boddoes go down it head-first.'

'Good ticket,' said Blotto fervently, his interest properly engaged. 'Not a job for limprags?'

'No, by Denzil. The kind of top-ranker who tackles the Croissant Run doesn't have any squidges about laying his life on the line.'

'Toad-in-the-hole!' said Blotto approvingly. 'Now you're

gabbing my kind of Japanese. So, you do get the odd coffination?'

'Not that many,' said Crocker. 'Maybe half a doz per annum.'

'This Croissant Run sounds like the lark's larynx,' Blotto enthused, his opinion of Switzerland improving by the minute. 'How soon can I get my boots in the irons?'

'I'll take you there to pop your peepers at it this very day,' said Crocker. 'Just one to-do to tick and then we'll pongle over there.' He looked up towards a figure approaching them on the balcony. 'And here is that to-do.'

The visitor was a stern-faced man with thick round glasses, who carried a voluminous black leather bag. When introduced to Blotto, he clicked his heels together, bowed snappily and announced himself to be: 'Herr Doktor Krankenschwindler.'

'Old pill-prescriber has come to get this gubbins off.' Crocker gestured towards his plastered leg.

And so Krankenschwindler set about his business. As he began, he said, in heavily accented English, 'I must be careful that it is only the plaster I remove and not the leg.' If this was an attempt at humour to calm any anxieties his patient might be feeling, the toneless delivery prevented it from having the desired effect. It sounded more like a threat.

The doctor used a saw. A long, thin saw with teeth set far apart, which actually looked as though it could be used for amputation as readily as plaster removal. But he knew what he was doing. With small, neat moves, he had soon cut lines down either side, so that the cast came apart like two halves of an Easter egg. The flesh revealed was pale and wrinkled, with vestiges of white bandage still adhering.

48

'These, Herr Wilmslow,' he said, 'will wash off in the bath. But it is very important that you follow my instructions for your continuing care until the fracture is fully healed. You must not stop using the crutches for another four weeks and take only minimal exercise. A few steps inside the hotel for two weeks, then allow yourself small excursions outside. A little more walking every day will help you to regain your strength. Do you understand what I'm saying, Herr Wilmslow?'

'Bong on the nose, Doc,' the patient assured him.

'And no attempts at any further winter sports for three months.'

'Three spoffing months it is, Mein Herr,' said Crocker with a mock salute.

Krankenschwindler turned to Blotto. 'As his friend, Herr Lyminster, I trust you will see to it that Herr Wilmslow follows my instructions. Will you undertake this task for me?'

'Tickey-tockey,' came the reply. 'Is the King German?'

While this expression was in common usage in the Land of the Golden Lions, it did cause slight confusion in Switzerland. But, once that had been sorted out, the doctor left.

'Righty-ho,' said Crocker Wilmslow. 'You wait here, Blotters me old fondue set. I'll dive into a bath, transform the toggings and be back with you as quick as a lizard's lick. Then we'll be on our way.'

The patient was off his chaise and speeding, crutchless, back into the hotel, before Blotto's words stopped him. '"On our way" where, Crockers me old sardine tin?'

'To the Croissant Run!' said Buffy 'Crocker' Wilmslow triumphantly.

'Heaven on a pickle-fork!' said Blotto approvingly.

* * *

49

Corky Froggett was at a loose end. He had survived the journey well, though being in France without being allowed to shoot anyone had been a bit of a trial. He missed the freedoms of wartime.

And, though Blotto had done most of the driving, he was pleased with the way the Lagonda had negotiated the icy roads and snowdrifts of the final leg, up the Altzberg mountain to Luzvimmen. The impression their arrival had made on the locals told him that cars were a rarity in the village. Clearly, the favoured method of transport was by horse-drawn sleigh.

Therein lay the cause of the looseness of Corky Froggett's end. The Hotel Luzvimmen did not even boast a garage, and the Lagonda was consigned to a dilapidated stable block, totally unsuitable accommodation for a creature of its pedigree. Even worse, it soon became clear that the young master and the young mistress would be using the local horse-drawn sleighs for any excursions they might take.

Corky didn't know much Shakespeare. If he had, he might have echoed The Moor of Venice's assertion that 'Othello's occupation's gone.' If he wasn't allowed to shoot people or to drive, then how was he going to survive in the icy dullness of Luzvimmen?

To add to his frustration, the stable where the Lagonda had ended up wasn't weatherproof. As soon as he had parked the beautiful monster there, Corky realised that, before he could begin his meticulous morning and evening routine of cleaning the vehicle, he would have to scrape the ice off. He hated to contemplate what long-term damage the deep frost might be inflicting on the hallowed bodywork.

And he hated to contemplate what long-term damage

the total dullness of Luzvimmen might be inflicting on his personality. He had suffered from boredom before. It was an unavoidable part of a chauffeur's life, sitting waiting until one's employers were ready to move. And he'd learnt to cope with that, to go into a state of suspended animation, a half-life from which he could snap out the moment the summons came.

He had also been royally bored in the army, but that was mitigated by the knowledge that one was about to go and shoot someone. He could not see any such bonuses to boredom in Luzvimmen.

So, the chauffeur's mind was full of gloomy prognostications the morning after their arrival, the day that Twinks would visit the Convent of the Sacred Icicle, the day that Blotto would meet Crocker Wilmslow on the hotel balcony.

Corky confronted the iced-up Lagonda in its stable. It had been with considerable difficulty that he had made the owner of his *pension* understand that he wanted a bucket of boiling water to start off his car-cleaning ritual. By the time he had got the bucket to the stable, the contents were only lukewarm and soon, he knew, they would be frozen solid, like everything else he had encountered in the bliss-bereft swamp-hole where fate had landed him.

Such was his frustration that, believing himself to be alone, Corky Froggett gave vent to a loud expletive. In English. (Well, actually, in a rather more historic form of English.)

He was shocked to receive a response. A heavily accented female voice from somewhere said, 'Good morning.'

He looked around and was gratified by the sight of a woman whose wrappings of fur disguised her actual contours but whose visible (deliberately visible?) cleavage suggested that she was constructed on generous lines.

51

Blonde pigtails emerged from her fur-lined hood and either the cold had brought a special glow to her cheeks, or they were the rosiest Corky had ever seen. An earthy wholesomeness emanated from her.

'Good morning,' he echoed.

'You,' said the woman, 'must be the chauffeur to the English couple who last night checked into the Hotel Luzvimmen.'

He could not deny the accuracy of her assessment. Nor was he that surprised that information spread so quickly in such a small village.

'And your name,' she went on, 'is Forky Croggett.'

'Not quite bong on the nose there,' he said, and gently corrected her.

'My name,' she announced, 'is Heidi Finnischann.'

'And how come you speak English, Miss Finnischann?'

'Please call me "Heidi".'

'Very well, Heidi. But how come you speak English?'

'I was governess to an English family. I taught their children Swiss German, Swiss French, and Swiss Italian. And skiing, of course.'

'And are you still working as a governess?'

'No, Forky. I—'

'Corky.'

'I am sorry. Corky. No, now, Corky, in the summer I work as a milkmaid. I take the cows to the pastures of the Altzberg, lulled by the sounds of their cowbells. And I milk them and look after them.'

'And in the winter?'

'In the winter, as well as looking after the cows down here, I work for Chäs Luzvimmen.'

'And who's he? Is "Chäs" short for "Charles"?'

'No, no. "Chäs Luzvimmen" is not a person. It is the

52

name of one of the biggest manufacturing companies in Switzerland.'

'Blimey!' said Corky. 'And what does it manufacture?'

'Cheese,' replied Heidi, with considerable pride.

'Cheese?' said Corky.

'Yes. Corky, did you by any chance have any cheese for breakfast at your *pension*?'

'Well, I was offered some,' he replied cautiously.

'Then that would definitely have been Chäs Luzvimmen,' said Heidi. 'Did you not think it tasted wonderful?'

'It looked wonderful,' said the chauffeur diplomatically. He wasn't about to tell her that he hadn't eaten any, because the cheese he'd been offered had been full of holes. Corky had been less than impressed by the standards of hygiene on display at the *pension*. It confirmed his instinctive distrust of foreigners. What kind of a guest house would leave cheese out where the mice could get at it?

Like the young master, Corky Froggett liked 'proper cheese', Cheddar with the consistency of soap.

'Chäs Luzvimmen, the company,' Heidi explained, 'is rapidly becoming one of the most successful of Swiss cheeses, rivalling Appenzeller, Emmental, Sbrinz, and even Gruyère. Everyone now recognises its distinctive red and yellow packaging. It is made up there.' She pointed towards the castle above the village, the one whose towers had pointy bits on top, rather than proper crenellations. 'That is where I milk the cows in the winter. They are housed in the lowest level of the building. Underground, where it used to be all dungeons. Some people say there still are a few dungeons there. I do not know. All I do know is that Schloss Luzvimmen has been converted into one of the most modern cheese making facilities in all of Switzerland.' She sounded suitably awestruck as she said this.

Corky Froggett felt confused. Having lived all his life in the shadow of Tawcester Towers, he assumed that all castles were designed to be loafed around in by aristocrats. The idea that one should be used for commercial purposes was alien – and rather distasteful – to him.

'So, what?' he asked Heidi. 'Did the family who inherited the castle sell up?'

'No,' she replied. 'They still live there.'

'And run a cheese factory?' asked an appalled Corky. He had heard the inhabitants of Tawcester Towers say often enough how inferior the aristocracy of all other countries were, but had never expected to hear of someone with a title making cheese.

He smiled at Heidi Finnischann. She returned him a full smile, full of infinite possibilities. The chauffeur was beginning to think that his sojourn in Luzvimmen might not be so boring, after all.

'So, who,' he asked, 'is this family who has fallen on such hard times that they have to make cheese?'

'They are an ancient line of Swiss aristocrats,' Heidi replied, 'called the von Strapp Family. And the one who has transformed Schloss Luzvimmen so successfully is the current Graf von Strapp.'

'Graf von Strapp?' echoed Corky.

'You know what a "Graf" is?'

'Yes, it's a sheet of squared paper on which mathematical information is recorded.'

'No, not that kind of "graph". Here in Switzerland, a "Graf" is a Count . . . you know, an aristocrat.'

'Ah, thank you. I understand. And so, the cheese factory up in the castle is run by Count von Strapp?'

'Yes, but that is not the name he is known by locally.'

'Oh, what's that then?'

Heidi Finnischann's rosy cheeks were wreathed in smiles as she replied, '"The Big Cheese".'

Buffy 'Crocker' Wilmslow had organised a horse-drawn sleigh to take them to the start of the Croissant Run. From there, only part of the rapid descent could be seen. The course had been designed by a former owner of the Hotel Luzvimmen. Using the natural contours of the mountainside, he had had earthworks erected to guide the Croissant Run's course. The basic shape was that of the pastry which gave the run its name, but within that curve there were many devious twists and switchbacks. With ice packed against floor and the sides, the surface of the chute had soon become too glassy for anything to stand on it except the metal runners of a toboggan.

Unfortunately, the original creator of the Croissant Run did not benefit from his innovation. He did everything right in developing the hotel and its attractions. He just did it too early, too soon after what Corky Froggett always referred to as 'the recent little dust-up in France'. The flood of winter-sports-loving English had yet to start. The result was that the proprietor went bankrupt and Hotel Luzvimmen was bought up (like much other property in the vicinity) by Count von Strapp. And he it was who profited from the growing popularity of the Croissant Run.

Of course, Blotto knew nothing of the sporting challenge's history. But Twinks had made it her business to find out all the details. She was particularly interested to learn the extent to which Count von Strapp was buying up all of the properties in Luzvimmen that he didn't already own. Economic power on that scale always intrigued her, because she had so often found that it involved criminality. She was keen to meet the Count and addressed her giant brain to the problem of organising such an encounter.

Blotto was surprised and pleased to find that, when he arrived at the start of the Croissant Run, he was ushered into a clubroom, whose interior felt reassuringly familiar. Its walls were covered with honours boards, listing the winning times of the various Croissant Run champions (along with one listing all those boneheaded heroes who had died in the attempt). There was also a blackboard on which were written in chalk the names of the most recent Croissant Runners and their times. It was just like being back at school.

This impression was increased by the fact that he recognised many of the names on the boards. And in the clubroom itself, he encountered – in the flesh – quite a few of his old muffin-toasters from Eton. They lounged around, in attitudes of aristocratic scruffiness, smoking pipes and quaffing, variously, local beer, wine and brandy.

Blotto's arrival prompted an inevitable welcome ritual, which was of course – as anyone who'd been at the old school would know – different from the one he'd exchanged with Buffy 'Crocker' Wilmslow. (Etiquette dictated this. With Crocker, it had been just the two of them. There was a variant protocol for the greeting of more than one Old Etonian.)

'Rackety-Rackety-Rackety!' the assembled throng intoned.

'Roo-Roo-Roo!' Blotto responded, right on cue.

56

'And are your sinews stiffened?' they asked, in unison.

'Tight as a pensioner's purse-strings!' came the required response.

'Rumble your rhubarb!' they cried.

'Rhubarb duly rumbled!' Blotto concluded.

The routine ended with a lot of mutual backslapping. Though an Eton education discouraged physical contact with another person unless you were fighting them, backslapping was permitted. And, indeed, the vigour with which backslapping was executed frequently made it indistinguishable from fighting.

The next business of the muffin-toasters was to decide who was to have the next go on the Croissant Run. There was much competition for this privilege, and the varied demands were assessed by someone who'd been an exact contemporary of Blotto at the old school. His name was Victor Muke-Wallingborough, known by everyone at Eton as 'Lewdie', a fine example of the logic prevailing in the award of adolescent nicknames. Victor Muke-Wallingborough's sobriquet owed nothing to any lewd tendencies he might have had. It was just that he excelled at all sports. So, benefiting from the gift of his first name, and the fact that the most successful athlete at a competition is known as the 'Victor Ludorum', the latter word was shortened and therefore 'Lewdie' was the only thing he could be called.

Blotto's relationship with this paragon was a wary one. Victor Muke-Wallingborough was the only one of his contemporaries who came close to matching his own sporting prowess. For a boddo at Eton to brag about himself was, of course, way the wrong side of the running rail, but Blotto did actually know that his athletic skills were superior to those of his rival. And, though in any one-on-one contest, it was he who actually triumphed, it was Muke-Wallingborough who got the nickname, 'Lewdie'.

Blotto sometimes wished that his first name had been 'Victor' rather than 'Devereux'.

So, in all dealings between the two old school-mates, there always existed an element of caution, not to say suspicion.

Blotto had noticed, the moment he arrived in the clubroom, that, at the top of the blackboard on which the recent best times were recorded, was chalked the name, 'V. J. de G. Muke-Wallingborough', with 1 minute 23.85 seconds. It became automatically a target to aim for and to beat.

As with any sporting challenge, Blotto was keen to have a go at the Croissant Run as soon as poss. But he recognised, being the new arrival on the scene, that there was probably some existing pecking order. Plenty of the other muffin-toasters in the clubroom were noisily offering their qualifications for next ride, but no one disagreed when Lewdie quietened them with a magisterial gesture and announced, 'You'll get your turn, chumbos, but I think the pot in this case should be handed on a silver salver to someone who has been unavoidably detained and unable to participate in our jollities for a couple of months. So, me old left-spiralling corkscrews, the next whizz at the wall cannot go to anyone other than our major muffin-toaster – Buffy "Crocker" Wilmslow!'

Everyone agreed his was a more persuasive claim than all the others. Crocker had, after all, been *hors de combat* for far too long. It was only fair biddles that a boddo in his sit should get first dibs on the 'boggan. And no one was happier with that decision than the recipient of the honour. 'Can't wait to get back on the old Croissant!' he cried gleefully.

With much raucous encouragement from his enthusiastic muffin-toasters, he was loaded face down onto the toboggan and given healthy shoves to speed him on his way.

Man and sledge went flying off the track at the first bend (the 'Widowmaker').

And Buffy 'Crocker' Wilmslow once again justified his nickname by breaking his right leg.

6

Leisure in Luzvimmen

Before he answered the question, Count von Strapp looked out from his fastness at the top of Schloss Luzvimmen. Though most of the windows in the building were narrow slits to frustrate besieging archers of long ago, one wall of his inner sanctum was a huge sheet of glass, commanding a panoramic view of the village of Luzvimmen, the hotel, the Convent of the Sacred Icicle, the Croissant Run clubroom, the yellow buildings in the foothills and the grandeur of adjacent mountains. The surrounding towers concealed this observation platform, so that it could not be seen from below.

The space was part office, part control room. The huge desk, behind which he faced the view from his throne-like chair, was backed by shelves full of ledgers and files and, in the middle of them, a high metal door. Along one wall was an array of brass-handled levers, switches and dials. Also, facing out over the rugged snow-covered landscape, were a couple of high-powered telescopes and two devices that looked suspiciously like machine guns.

Count von Strapp, a man whose main features were

his eyebrows – so large and bristling that they required topiary – relished the dominance of his position. Schloss Luzvimmen had been in his family for generations, but he prided himself on being the first holder of the title who had realised the place's full potential. He held the keys to more sources of power than his ancestors could ever have dreamt of.

The Count relished power in every form. He relished the power he was exercising at that moment, taking his time to answer the question his visitor had just put to him. He knew that Ulrich Weissfeder was far too aware of his lowly position to repeat it or attempt to prompt him. The hotelier humbly awaited his superior's response.

Which Count von Strapp finally granted. 'No,' he said. 'I have not heard of Lord Devereux or Lady Honoria Lyminster.'

'They are sometimes known,' said Weissfeder, 'as "Blotto and Twinks".'

The Count shuddered. 'Even less have I ever had – or wished to have – the acquaintance of persons called "Blotto and Twinks".'

'I came across them – brother and sister they are – when I was working in England. Their family seat is called Tawcester Towers, in the county of Tawcestershire.'

'Of what interest is this information to me?' asked the Count irritably. The eyebrows bristled even more aggressively.

'It is of interest, Eure Exzellenz,' the hotelier replied smoothly, 'because the two young people are not what they seem. During my sojourn at Tawcester Towers, it became clear that they are English spies.'

'How do you know this, Weissfeder?'

'I know it because they foiled a plan devised by none other than The Crooked Hand.'

Count von Strapp was impressed. Along with their intense rivalry, international criminal masterminds with plans for world domination tend to have professional respect for each other. 'I heard that The Crooked Hand's operation had been brought to an end, but I did not know how that happened.'

'I can assure you, sir, that it was the work of Blotto and Twinks.' The Count winced. The hotelier quickly corrected himself. 'Lord Devereux and Lady Honoria Lyminster.'

'Hmm.' Count von Strapp ran his fingers thoughtfully through the herbage of his eyebrows. 'And what, Weissfeder, is the ostensible explanation for the sudden appearance of these two English spies in Luzvimmen?'

'Lady Honoria claims to be here to investigate the disappearance of a friend's sister from the Convent of the Sacred Icicle.'

'She wouldn't be the first to have disappeared from there.'

'No, Eure Exzellenz. But I believe the real purpose of their visit is something far more important than finding a missing schoolgirl.'

'Clarify what you mean, Weissfeder.'

'What, Eure Exzellenz, is there here on the Altzberg mountain that poses a threat to the safety of international relations, that in fact could threaten world peace?'

'Ah.' The Count nodded. 'You think what interests them is the operation that I am preparing here at Schloss Luzvimmen?'

'That is exactly what I think, Eure Exzellenz,' said Ulrich Weissfeder.

'Which means they might be spies working for the

nameless person who is determined to thwart my plans for world domination?'

'You mean "Wilhelm Tell"?'

The eyebrows bristled furiously. 'I said "nameless"! There are cruel and unusual punishments reserved for people who mention that name in Schloss Luzvimmen!'

'Forgive me, Eure Exzellenz,' said Weissfeder cravenly. 'I was not using my head.'

'After the cruel and unusual punishments reserved for you, you will not have a head to lose!'

'Please, Eure Exzellenz. Please forgive my thoughtlessness.'

There was a long silence. Behind his eyebrows, Count von Strapp was unhappy. The mention of Wilhelm Tell's name had brought unpleasant recollections to him. He had never met the person in question, nor indeed encountered anyone who'd met him. The man who had taken on that name, which was so heavily weighted with Swiss history, acted undercover. Nobody knew his real identity or where he was based. But the Count was convinced his enemy had a knack of recruiting followers so loyal to him that they would put into action any atrocity that their leader demanded of them.

Many people in Switzerland did not believe in the reincarnated Wilhelm Tell. They dismissed him as a figment of gullible folk imagination. Count von Strapp knew better. He reckoned that Wilhelm Tell was the only serious rival he had in his search for world domination. It was a thought that kept him awake at nights.

'I will show mercy to you on this occasion, Weissfeder,' he said, ending the hotelier's agony, 'but don't dare do that again!'

'I will swear on any sacred thing you wish me to swear on that I will not commit the same offence again.'

'Very well, then. Swear on "Chäs Luzvimmen".'

'I swear, on Chäs Luzvimmen, that I will never again mention the unnamed one in Schloss Luzvimmen.'

The Count seemed content with that. An icy shudder ran down Ulrich Weissfeder's back as he realised how close he had come to destruction.

'So, Weissfeder, you think that the two new arrivals at your hotel might be spies for the one we do not give a name to?'

'It is possible, Eure Exzellenz.'

'Strange that they should come from England . . .' the Count mused. Then paranoia struck him. International criminal masterminds with plans for world domination have notoriously thin skins. 'Perhaps the range of operations for the one whose name is not to be spoken have extended as far as England . . . ? Perhaps I should start building my network up there too?'

'I don't think you need to, Eure Exzellenz. From my experience of living in the country, the English show no interest in world domination. They assume, mistakenly, that they have achieved it already.'

'Hm.' The haunted glint in Count von Strapp's eye subsided. 'So, what would you recommend I should do, Weissfeder?'

'I would recommend that you meet Lady Honoria.'

'Just her? Not the brother?'

'She is the important one. The fact is, Eure Exzellenz, that the siblings have only one brain between them. And it's all hers. Lord Devereux's brain compares unfavourably with the void between the horns of the milking cows in the dungeons of Schloss Luzvimmen.'

64

'Very well, Weissfeder. Arrange a meeting for me with Lady Honoria.'

'Immediately, Eure Exzellenz.'

People who live in cold climates soon develop heat-seeking antennae, and Heidi Finnischann, having spent her entire life in Luzvimmen, was no exception. She had worked with cows since early childhood and knew how much warmth they could generate. She spent her summers with them on the Altzberg mountain pastures, lulled by the tolling of their bells, but she also sought out their company during the winter season, because they spent that on the ground floor of her parents' chalet. There they munched blissfully on the hay that her farmer father had spent the summer cutting. And the heat of their bodies provided an efficient form of central heating for the house.

The cows' accommodation also provided a very comfortable private area for Heidi and anyone she chose to share it with. The hay was stacked in a partitioned-off section of the ground-floor cowshed, one side of which opened to allow access to a pitchfork which would gather the beasts' daily rations. And the surface of the hay store provided a bower as soft as any feather bed.

Lest anyone should think that the atmosphere in the cows' quarters might be sullied by the products of their natural bodily functions, it should be pointed out that Heidi Finnischann kept everything scrupulously clean. Her charges were milked morning and night and, because their milk was drunk or turned to cheese for her family, high standards of hygiene had to be maintained.

Having a generous soul and an abundantly welcoming body, Heidi Finnischann had often shared her hayrick hideaway with chosen friends, amongst whose list Corky Froggett found himself honoured to be included. And, as they lay on the hay in satisfied torpor that afternoon, he asked her about the winter work she did at Schloss Luzvimmen.

'It is the same,' she said, 'as the work I do here. I look after cows.'

'Ah.'

'Production on the scale that operates at Chäs Luzvimmen requires an enormous amount of milk. All of the cellars – what used to be the dungeons – of Schloss Luzvimmen are full of cows, and I am one of many milk-maids whose task it is to milk them morning and night.'

'And do those cows also go out on to the mountain pastures in the summer?'

'No, they spend the entire year in the Schloss. That way they are more productive. They are fed on a special diet, developed by the Graf von Strapp – that is, the Count von Strapp, as you would say it.'

'Isn't it cruel to keep the cows inside all year round?'

'No, it is not cruel,' said Heidi, a little miffed at potential criticism of the business practices of Chäs Luzvimmen. 'It is efficient. Maximum efficiency is always the aim of the Count von Strapp. He has the most modern of equipment and is constantly developing new machinery. That is why his company has exceeded the results of all other Swiss cheesemakers. Soon there will be no Appenzeller, Emmental, Sbrinz or Gruyère. They will all cease to be produced as their firms go bankrupt. The only Swiss cheese available will be Chäs Luzvimmen!'

Though no one could be a more passionate advocate for loyalty to one's employer, Corky was taken aback by the vehemence of Heidi Finnischann's assertions. If this was the kind of allegiance which Count von Strapp demanded from his staff, then he was clearly a forceful personality.

He was about to ask more about the mysterious Count, but Heidi, responding to the sound of the church clock, said that she must check into Schloss Luzvimmen for the evening milking.

Corky Froggett returned to his *pension* with a smile beneath his fiercely bristling moustache. The prospects for his stay in Luzvimmen had improved considerably since that morning.

Twinks had frequently found that lack of progress on one intellectual problem could be alleviated, not by worrying away at it, but by focusing on something else entirely. It was for that reason that, with headway stalled on her search for Aurelia ffrench-Windeau, she turned the power of her mighty brain on to one of her translation projects.

She always had one or two on the go to keep the mind tuned up. Her current challenge was making a Korean version of *Charley's Aunt* (something which – remarkably to her mind – no one had ever attempted before). She had not embarked on it with a view to Brandon Thomas's famous farce being produced in Korea. Twinks had a proper aristocratic contempt for the commercial world. Her class's view of money was that it should either be inherited or stolen from exploited foreigners (or, very frequently, both). Her translation was of value to her only as an intellectual exercise, and hopefully as a means of animating back-burner thoughts on the Aurelia ffrench-Windeau problem.

As a venue to work on it, she had rejected the option of her bedroom and chosen the Hotel Luzvimmen's library. It seemed to be permanently people-free. Since most of the guests were the kind of winter-sports enthusiasts who Blotto had met at the Croissant Run clubroom, reading did not feature high – if at all – on their priority lists. Since the only books in the library were in English, Twinks had no Swiss library users to disturb her concentration. She checked out the contents of the shelves. There were a few volumes of local tourist information, folk myths and that kind of thing, but most of the books were about skiing, skating and tobogganing.

(The presence of these English skiing manuals showed that the management thought they knew where their market was. In fact, they'd miscalculated. The kind of Old Etonians attracted to winter sports would have thought it *infra dig* to be seen reading a book on the subject. Blotto's muffin-toasters shared his own view that reading books on how to play games was almost as far beyond the barbed wire as actually training for them. Only Americans – and probably solicitors – were crass enough to do that.)

Out of interest – and because of what Sister Benedicta had said in the Convent of the Sacred Icicle – Twinks took from the shelf a book on the history and folklore of Wilhelm Tell. She slipped it into her sequined reticule to read another time, and concentrated on the challenges of translation.

She was in the process of finding the right light-hearted Korean idiom for one of Charley's Aunt's most famous phrases, 'Brazil – where the nuts come from', when the library door opened to admit a particularly obsequious Ulrich Weissfeder.

'Lady Honoria . . .' he began silkily.

'Yes?' she said, moving straight into her mother's most peremptory manner. Given the circumstances of their last encounter, she felt no obligation to follow her customary rule of politeness to underlings.

'I come with an invitation for you, milady.'

Her 'Oh?' was as frosty as the weather outside.

'I don't know if you happen to know, but there is a castle near this village.'

'Yes. Schloss Luzvimmen. And of what interest is that to me?'

'Schloss Luzvimmen is owned by—'

'It's owned by the Graf von Strapp. I know that.'

Ulrich Weissfeder was encountering the disadvantages, which many before him had come up against, of talking to someone who literally knew everything. 'It is from the Graf von Strapp that the invitation comes,' he said.

'Ah.' For the first time, there was a tinge of interest in Twinks's voice.

'The Count wishes to invite you – and your brother, if available – to share the hospitality of Schloss Luzvimmen.'

This prompted an even more positive 'Ah.' Any information about what went on in Luzvimmen might prove helpful in her search for Aurelia ffrench-Windeau.

'That is very gracious of the Count,' she announced, restored to her usual aristocratic *politesse*. 'Inform him that I – and my brother – would be delighted to accept his invitation.'

Though her mind had the objective sharpness of a scalpel when assessing evidence, Twinks was also a great believer in the unexpected power of serendipity. The problem of arranging a meeting with Count von Strapp had been magically solved.

* * *

69

The said brother was, at the time she was speaking, still at the clubroom by the start of the Croissant Run. Buffy 'Crocker' Wilmslow had once again been taken off into the care of Doktor Krankenschwindler, to be berated for ignoring the worthy physician's advice. The encroaching evening meant that soon it would be time for the last Croissant Run of the day, and Victor Muke-Wallingborough had insisted that the honour of taking it should be granted to the Luzvimmen's most recent arrival, Devereux Lyminster.

Blotto knew exactly what was going on. Though Lewdie's offer had been couched in the most generous of terms and presented as a great favour, it was born of their historic Old Etonian rivalry. Lewdie knew that Blotto could not resist a challenge, and the thought of humiliating him before his muffin-toasters in a difficult discipline he had never tried before was too attractive to pass up. Secure in his currently dominant time of 1 minute 23.85 seconds, Victor Muke-Wallingborough just could not wait to see his rival fail.

Of course, Blotto agreed. From the Battle of Hastings onwards, no Lyminster had ever turned down a challenge. He took minimum notice of the basic guidelines given to him by one of the skiing instructors who specialised in toboggan training, and rejected the offer of protective clothing. The tweed suit he was wearing had survived worse conditions. His only regret was that he hadn't brought his cricket bat with him. He was determined to have it with him the next time he came to the Croissant Run.

All attempts on the 'boggan challenge were timed by a man with a stopwatch at the bottom of the run. His cue to start the watch came from the switching on of a red light high on a pole above the clubroom.

Blotto was a natural athlete. The toboggan may have been an unfamiliar piece of kit, but he grabbed it with both hands and trusted to providence. (Providence, over the years, had always seemed to have a soft spot for Blotto.) His time for his first attempt at the Croissant Run was 1 minute 17.31 seconds.

Of course, he didn't crow over his rival. Boddoes who'd been muffin-toasters at Eton just didn't do that sort of thing. On his return to the clubroom, all he did was shrug sheepishly and say, 'Beginner's luck.'

But he couldn't hold back a smile when the scorer rubbed out Lewdie's championship time and chalked in Blotto's.

Victor Muke-Wallingborough was absolutely furious.

7

The Big Cheese

After his triumph on the Croissant Run, Blotto returned to Hotel Luzvimmen to the news from his sister that they were expected that evening as guests of Count von Strapp at Schloss Luzvimmen. Though he would have preferred to stay in, testing out the local beers, wines and liqueurs, Blotto knew better than to cross Twinks. If she told him there was something that needed doing, then he did it. Having grown up at Tawcester Towers with the Dowager Duchess of Lyminster, he knew that no boddo who wanted to keep his ears unbent ever argued with a woman.

Twinks arranged that one of the hotel's horse-drawn sleighs would deliver them to the Schloss at the appointed hour.

The ground floor gave no hint that the ancient building had now been converted into a cheese factory. They were admitted, by passive, black-uniformed servants, whose loose tunics and tight black caps covering all their hair left their gender debatable.

Blotto and Twinks were ushered through the vast metal-studded external doors into a cavernous hallway, illuminated by flaming torches in sconces. Huge logs crackled in monumental fireplaces on either side. The walls were covered with displays of ancient armour, fanned-out lances, halberds and captured banners. Though Schloss Luzvimmen was obviously much inferior to Tawcester Towers, there were elements of this style of décor that were familiar to the visiting siblings. The trappings of war have an international currency.

The style of dress adopted by their host, however, was not at all familiar. At his appearance, there was an immediate drop of Blotto's chin (he was lucky among his fellow Old Etonians in actually having one). And the shock didn't arise from the fact that Count von Strapp's face was mostly eyebrow. It was his clothes. He was dressed in leather shorts with a bib attached, a fashion that Blotto had never seen outside a nursery. It was only a very sharp dig in the ribs from his sister's elbow that stopped him from making some unsuitable comment.

'*Wilkommen in meinem,*' said the Count expansively. Then, in English, 'Welcome ... What should I call you? Lord Devereux and Lady Honoria?'

'Blotto and Twinks is fine,' said Twinks. 'That is what all our chumbos call us.'

'Well, I would be honoured to be included in the list of your chumbos,' Count von Strapp lied. His English was good but heavily accented. Of course, Twinks could have conversed with him in Swiss German, but that would have left her brother in a thicker fog of incomprehension than the one he normally inhabited.

What Blotto did notice, however, because he had become so familiar with it over the years, was the immediate effect

73

his sister had on the Count. Men fell for Twinks like mid-shipmen dropping from crow's nests, and the Swiss cheese magnate was no exception. Beneath their copious brows, his eyes were visibly popping out. Twinks, as ever, was either unaware of or uninterested in the phenomenon.

'First,' said the Count, once he had partially recovered his equilibrium, 'we will have refreshments. Then I will give you a tour of the most technologically advanced factory in the whole of Europe, probably the whole of the world.'

This proposal suited Twinks fine. She was intrigued to know what Count von Strapp was up to in Schloss Luzvimmen. Her highly sensitive antennae suspected that there was more to it than met the eye; that there was in fact something illegal about his operation.

They were led up by more black-uniformed flunkies to a state room on the castle's first floor. This too was lit by flaming torches, and the space was dominated by another vast open fireplace.

'I suppose,' Blotto commented to the Count, 'you boddoes up here don't have the whole clangdumble of electricity. Too far to drag up the fumacious wires, I dare say . . . ?'

'I can assure you,' said Count von Strapp, the rest of his body bristling as much as his eyebrows, 'that we have a highly efficient electrical system in Luzvimmen. And I should know, because it is I who created and developed it. I have put Switzerland at the head of the world in hydro-electric technology . . .' he smiled pityingly '. . . but I'm sure neither of you know what hydroelectric technology is.'

The blankness on Blotto's face suggested that, in his case, this assumption was correct, but his sister intervened smoothly. 'The world's first hydroelectric project was organised in 1878 by the industrial magnate William Armstrong, later First Baron Armstrong, at Cragside, the house he built near the Northumberland town of Rothbury. It was the first building to be lit by electricity provided by hydropower. At Cragside, Armstrong also used home-generated electricity to power a sawmill, a laundry, a dishwasher, an elevator and a rotisserie.

'The first commercial application of the new energy source came in 1882, when a plant was installed in Appleton, Wisconsin in the United States. It was quickly followed by . . .'

Twinks proceeded to take her narrative through many other developments, even going back to the important pioneering work of Johann Segner, Jean-Victor Poncelet, Benoît Fourneyron and James B. Francis on water turbines, then coming more up to date with the 1895 Edward Dean Adams Power Plant at Niagara Falls and the 1905 Chinese hydroelectric station on the Xindian Creek near Taipei.

Count von Strapp had just learnt the inadvisability of assuming ignorance in Twinks. On any subject. But someone who thought as much of himself as the Count did was not going to be cast down by his error. 'I am, you must understand, one of the foremost scientific minds in the whole of Europe, probably the whole of the world. Though what you have seen of Schloss Luzvimmen so far may make you think it is run on a primitive pre-electrical system, that is misleading. In these reception rooms, my aim is to capture the romantic grandeur of an earlier age.

'The Switzerland of today is a pale facsimile of the Switzerland of old. For our country the Middle Ages were a time of chivalry, a time when knights in armour travelled around righting wrongs. But those attitudes have been corrupted by bourgeois complacency. And *neutrality*.' He spoke the word with hatred.

'We used to be a noble, warlike nation. I am determined

that Switzerland will return to those former values! Values of honesty, justice, mutual tolerance and respect for one's fellow man! And I am prepared to kill anyone who does not support those values!'

The shrillness of his voice towards the end of this oration acted as a warning to Twinks. It was the sound of the fanatic. Count von Strapp was one of those megalomaniacs who believed that any level of violence was permissible in pursuit of his principles. Such men, she knew all too well, were dangerous.

His anger reminded the Count of his suspicions of the two visitors. He wanted to return to an earlier and better time in Switzerland, but rumour had it that his nemesis, the one he was not prepared to give a name to, wanted to regress even further. To the fourteenth century, when the exploits of the hero whose name he'd taken were first recorded.

'Do you,' he asked with all the coolness he could muster, 'know much about someone called Wilhelm Tell . . . ?'

'I do, actually,' said Blotto, to the considerable surprise of his sister. Stirrings of memory from the beaks at Eton came back to him. 'An apple was part of the whole flip-madoodle, wasn't it?'

'Yes, it was,' the Count concurred.

'All comes back to me.'

Twinks looked at her brother in amazement to see what would come back to him. 'Wilhelm Tell and the apple. Wilhelm Tell sat under a tree, an apple dropped on him and he also invented gravy.'

'Gravity?' Twinks suggested diffidently.

'Tickey-tockey, that's the Johnny!' said Blotto.

The Count relaxed. If that was the level of intellect he was up against, he didn't feel too threatened. Surely, the one whose name is not to be spoken would have gone for a higher level of competence in his spies.

Unless, of course, Blotto was employing an elaborate double bluff . . . ? Count von Strapp looked at the patrician face in front of him to assess this possibility. But no. Though honest and undoubtedly good-looking, the man he saw didn't look capable of dealing even with a single one.

The sister, though . . . As Ulrich Weissfeder had warned him, she was the one with the majority of the siblings' shared brain. She might be more troublesome. He would keep a closer eye on her.

But, for the time being, he went back to his impersonation of a generous host. 'The refreshments I am offering you now bear witness to my technological innovations. I am serving you *Eiswein*, produced from grapes frozen while they were still on the vine. Making this wine has in the past been a slow and laborious process, but I have refined the method, which enables me to produce the glorious nectar at a speed that cannot be matched by my rivals. Nor can the quality of my *Eiswein* be matched by my rivals. It is the finest wine in the whole of Europe, probably the whole of the world.'

Clearly this was a catchphrase for him. If he appeared in music halls back in the Land of the Golden Lions, Twinks reflected, the posters would feature those words between his first name and his surname. She didn't know his first name but, mentally, she had him down as a 'Gunter'. She had a mental image of the playbill: 'Gunter "in the whole of Europe, probably the whole of the world" von Strapp'. That'd bring the punters in. Or possibly not.

'And,' the Count went on grandiloquently, 'the cheese you are being offered has been made by a new up-to-date method which I personally have developed. I am confident, when you taste it, you will agree that it is the finest cheese in the whole of Europe, probably the whole of the world!

'What is more, all of this is powered by the most sophisticated hydroelectric system in the whole of Europe, probably the whole of the world! I will give you a tour of my mechanical installations, just as soon as you have finished your refreshments.'

Under normal circumstances, Blotto would have rather resented this urging not to spend too long on refreshments. Back at receptions at Tawcester Towers, he tended to linger until he'd emptied the last bottle of champagne and eaten the last quail's egg with celery salt. But he wasn't that keen on what was on offer at Schloss Luzvimmen. The *Eiswein* was so sweet that each sip seemed to take a layer off his teeth. He longed for the robust comfort of the club claret at The Gren.

And, as for the cheese . . .

Each slice was peppered with holes like a paper target fired at by a less good marksman than Blotto was (which actually included everyone in the world – no one could match him for marksmanship). The thought invaded the customary vacuity of his brain that Swiss cheese was not only an assault on the tastebuds, but also a potential cause of criminality. When a Swiss cheese-seller weighed out half a pound of the stuff, Blotto reasoned, the poor deluded customers didn't realise that half of what they were paying for were holes.

He felt very pleased with himself. He always did when he came up with an unarguable piece of logic like that. It put in their place people who questioned the power of his intellect. Or even whether he had one. The Swiss system of cheese-selling, he concluded, went against every law of cricket.

The Count had told them that the ground-floor level of Schloss Luzvimmen was in a different style from the rest, but they hadn't expected quite such a contrast as was revealed when, accompanied by two of the black-uniformed servants, they stepped out of the hydro-electrically powered elevator on the next floor up. Gone were the torches in sconces, gone were the displays of armour and heraldic banners. In their place stood huge vats whose contents rumbled with bubbling. Vertical and horizontal copper piping threaded along the walls and ceiling. Pumps sighed and groaned. The overpowering smell was of cheese, but not a pleasant cheese. There were hints of that vomit aroma that always accompanies Parmesan.

The huge space, part factory, part laboratory, was a hive of industry. Its worker bees were dressed in white versions of the uniforms worn by the downstairs servants. Again, loose tops and tight headdresses disguised their gender into a kind of impersonal neutrality. They scurried around unceasingly, knowing the precise definition of their tasks and fulfilling them without question or pause.

Count von Strapp spread his arms wide to encompass the entire industrial scene. 'Here,' he said, perhaps predictably, 'you see the most advanced machinery in the whole of Europe, probably the whole of the world!'

'Spoffing impressive load of gubbins,' said Blotto, also looking round. Then adding hopefully, 'Can it do anything apart from making cheese?'

For a moment, the Count looked uncertain. 'What kind of other thing do you believe it might make?'

'I don't know. Any old rombooley. Just seems a rather big paraphernatus just to make spoffing cheese.'

Was Twinks being oversensitive to spot an ingredient of relief in von Strapp's expression of response to her brother's words? Was it possible that Blotto had inadvertently touched on a truth – that the factory actually was producing something other than cheese? Food for thought.

'Why, in the name of St Bernard,' asked the Count with bluff insouciance, 'would anyone want to do anything apart from making cheese?'

Blotto was about to say, 'Because of the horracious taste', but a sharp look from his sister, who could read his mind like a book (a children's book, to be fair) told him it wasn't the moment. Instead, he asked, 'And has this advanced machinery solved your problem?'

'What problem? We do not have a problem.'

'I'm sorry to put crud in your crumpet,' said Blotto politely, 'but you do have something of a rat in the larder here. Every chunk of cheese that comes out of your flip-madoodle has blimping great holes in it. And if that's not the stickiest end of the paint pot, then I'm an Apache dancer!'

Though Count von Strapp had not met Blotto before, he seemed quickly to have attuned to the idea that there were times when engaging in discussion with the young man was not advisable. This he clearly reckoned to be one of those occasions. Instead of responding to what had just been said, he continued his guided tour. Pointing up to the vast rumbling vats, he addressed his words to Twinks. His manner veered between the boastful and the obsequious, a mixture she had seen played out many times before from men trying at the same time to impress and to show their sensitive side. (Incidentally, it never worked.)

'What is revolutionary about my cheese-manufacturing system,' said the Count, 'is the means of delivery of the product. Particularly given the location of my factory here, a less brilliant entrepreneur than myself might waste a lot of money in organising transport to come up the mountain to collect the finished rounds of cheese. The expenditure on horse-drawn sleighs up here and petrol-driven vans in the foothills would be exorbitant and cut severely into the profits of Chäs Luzvimmen.

'But my genius has seen a way around this problem. Take a look at this junction in the piping here . . .' He indicated the bottom of one of the vats, to which was attached a large funnel-shaped tube, rather like the horn of a gramophone. From the narrower end, a thick brass pipe led along the factory floor until it disappeared through the castle wall. 'This conduit goes down the mountainside, tracing the path of an ancient glacier and at one point following the contours of the Croissant Run, where young English idiots enjoy breaking their bones. It is through this pipeline that the cheese flows, while still in a melted and liquid state, so that it can be treated at the foot of the mountain, where the temperature is warmer. You might have noticed the processing works down there from your car when you first arrived.'

Twinks had, of course, observed the yellow buildings from the back of the Lagonda and immediately identified them as cheese-processing installations. Blotto, needless to say, had been totally unaware of them.

'So,' the Count went on, 'all of the maturing processes for the cheese, the storing, the packing, the transportation to all the markets of the world, though controlled from Schloss Luzvimmen, is in fact conducted from those buildings at the foot of the Altzberg mountain.

'In this fashion,' said the Count, by now heady with self-praise, 'I save money in a way my competitors can only dream of. They cannot begin to match my business acumen. The names of Appenzeller, Emmental, Sbrinz, and even Gruyère will soon be forgotten for ever. And the only Swiss cheese available will be Chäs Luzvimmen. Produced by the most efficient factory in the whole of Europe, probably the whole of the world!

'Soon, everyone will acknowledge the supreme genius of Count von Strapp!'

The shrillness Twinks had noticed earlier was back in his voice. It made her nervous. The ambitions of such a fanatic could surely not be restricted to the world of cheese? He must have darker and more cosmic plans.

But he was also clearly someone who knew everything about the doings of Luzvimmen. Indeed, he seemed to own most of the place. Twinks would be wasting an opportunity if she didn't question him about the main purpose of her visit to Switzerland.

'Tell me,' she cut in on his self-aggrandisement, 'what do you know about the Convent of the Sacred Icicle?'

He was so taken aback by the sudden change of subject that he just mouthed blankly for a moment, before asking, 'Why? You have no plans to join it, do you?'

'By Wilberforce, no! Becoming a nun is certainly not my length of banana. But I'm trying to join up the links with the sister of an old chumbo of mine. The little droplet was sent out to the Convent of the Sacred Icicle to be finished.'

'"To be finished"?' echoed the Count. 'You mean to be terminated?' His brow – or what could be seen of it through the eyebrows – clouded. 'It would not be the first time such an event has happened in that place.'

'No, no, you've popped the wrong partridge!' said Twinks. 'Your country has a juicy repu for its finishing schools, where young feminine thimbles from England have the rough edges sanded off them and are shaped into suitable marriage fodder. After the treatment, they are perfectly set up to twiddle the old reef-knot with chinless scions of the lesser aristocracy, and thereafter live lives of indolent leisure on the family jingle-jangle.'

'Ah, *ja.*' Count von Strapp nodded. 'I have heard of such activities at the convent. The training of young girls. But I had not heard that they were being trained for marriage.'

'Then what, in the name of ginger, have you heard they are being trained for?'

'It is not of importance.'

'Yes, it is, by Denzil! And, not to fiddle round the fir trees, what have you heard about young girls being "terminated" at the Convent of the Sacred Icicle? Do you mean "coffinated"?'

'I have no further information on that subject,' came the curt reply. Evidently, Twinks's questioning had crossed some invisible line with the Count.

But she persisted. 'Do you know the denizens of the spoffing Convent of the Sacred Icicle? They tried to shudder me off on my first visitette. But, if they think they can put the frighteners on me, they're shimmying up the wrong drainpipe. We Lyminsters don't scare that easily.'

'I'm sure you don't,' said the Count unctuously. 'But, if I am reading your intentions correctly, Twinks, you are asking if I know another means of gaining access to the Convent of the Sacred Icicle, other than by using the front doors?'

'You're bong on the nose, Count. You read my semaphore exactly.'

'In that case, I can supply your wants exactly.' The Count snapped his fingers to attract one of the black-uniformed servants and whispered instructions in his (or her) ear. The man (or woman) scurried off as his (or her) beaming master turned back to his beautiful guest. 'When you leave Schloss Luzvimmen this evening, you will be given an envelope containing precise details of how to gain clandestine access to the Convent of the Sacred Icicle.'

'Thank you,' said Twinks graciously. 'You're a Grade A foundation stone.' She didn't really think this Swiss cheese-maker deserved quite such a high accolade, but she knew the usages of polite society, which obtained even in Europe.

'Now,' said the Count with great enthusiasm, 'would you like me to take you down the mountain to see the processing plants?'

Blotto and Twinks exchanged covert glances. Neither could think of anything they'd like to do less but, as ever, brother relied on sister to come up with a polite way out of the situation.

'That's very kind, Count,' she said in a voice of shimmering charm, 'but I think our senses are too full of admiration for what we have seen up here to accommodate further excitements this evening.'

'Well, if you're sure . . .' said the Count.

'Yes, we are,' Twinks responded with marked firmness. She went on, with an insincerity that Count von Strapp was far too self-absorbed to recognise, 'We are most grateful to you for showing us the creations of your genius.'

The Count preened himself under the flattery, as she went on: 'Clearly, you have produced the finest cheese ever seen in the whole of Europe, probably the whole of the world.'

Even though the stuff's full of fumacious holes, thought Blotto savagely.

8

The Fate of Spies

In the horse-drawn sleigh which took them back to Hotel Luzvimmen, Blotto didn't pass any comment on the envelope which his sister had been handed on departure. Instead, he moaned on about the inadequacies of a country that couldn't even produce unperforated cheese.

'I mean, do they put blimping holes in everything?' he asked despairingly. 'If so, you wouldn't catch me risking my chitterlings in one of their aeroplanes.'

In this mood, Blotto didn't need any responses to his dialogue and Twinks gave him none. She was preoccupied with the contents of the envelope she was holding, caught between gratitude to Count von Strapp for helping her mission and suspicions about his reasons for doing so. She hadn't forgotten his momentary, quickly covered, reaction when Blotto had asked whether his factory could make anything other than cheese. The Count's ill-disguised fanaticism had made Twinks extremely wary of him.

'I mean,' her brother went on, 'imagine if they had spoffing holes in the parachutes too? If the aeroplane went down because it'd got ghastible holes in it, and then the parachute that was meant to stop you being coffinated also had holes in it . . . well, you'd be lined up for a quick trip to the Pearlies with no time off for good behaviour, wouldn't you?'

Again, Twinks maintained her silence.

When they got back to Hotel Luzvimmen, Blotto wandered into the bar where he met some of his new friends from the Croissant Run. They had discovered that the hotel cellars contained a perfectly acceptable French claret. Not up to the one at The Gren, obviously, but perfectly acceptable.

There was a strange moment when they first ordered the wine. The bar staff asked if they wanted to drink it as *Glühwein*. Once the muffin-toasters had had it explained to them what this was, their cries of derision were loud. As Blotto asked, 'What kind of slugbucket would want to ruin a perfectly acceptable claret by heating it up?'

Once that wrinkle had been ironed out, he was able to take away the sticky taste of the dreaded *Eiswein* and get quietly wobbulated with his old muffin-toasters.

Twinks, meanwhile, took her precious envelope up to the privacy of her bedroom.

Fresh from pleasant diversions in Heidi Finnischann's hayloft, Corky Froggett found himself asking idly about Count von Strapp. The awe with which she had spoken of her employer suggested that he was a person of some interest.

'From what you say about him, it sounds as if he has a very big operation up in the castle, if it's just for making cheese.'

'Who says it is just for making cheese?'

'That's what you suggested, Heidi.'

'No, no, that is only part of his manufacturing process. He is also doing much research into other subjects. The Graf von Strapp is one of the foremost experimental scientists in the whole of Europe, probably the whole of the world!'

Corky was not to know that the milkmaid was actually quoting her employer at that point.

'He is always developing new ideas,' Heidi went on. 'As well as the laboratories where he refines the cheesemaking processes, there are other laboratories which are kept securely locked and in which the Graf conducts other experiments.'

'And do you know what is the purpose of these other experiments?'

'No, Corky. Nobody knows that. What goes on in there is a closely guarded secret. But, given the Count's philanthropic nature, I am sure it is all done for the good of humanity.'

Not necessarily convinced by her last sentence, the chauffeur salted away the piece of information. It might be of interest to the young master. Or, more likely, to the young mistress.

He was about to go and defrost the Lagonda yet again. But Heidi delayed him with her blandishments.

And, it had to be said, she did have very nice blandishments.

'Well, I can see you are in a bit of a fumacious gluepot,' said Blotto.

It was hard to deny the truth of this observation. Buffy 'Crocker' Wilmslow was bedbound in Luzvimmen's tiny sanatorium, which was actually adjacent to the Convent of the Sacred Icicle and staffed by nuns from that institution.

Crocker was different from the other patients. All the rest were suffering from tuberculosis, undergoing a regime which involved having windows wide open to let in the healing Swiss air. Crocker, his plaster-covered right leg suspended in a cradle over his bed, was not appreciating the cold. But, when he remonstrated with them, the nuns behaved as if closing any windows was an offence to their religion.

'You're bong on the nose there, Blotters,' said Crocker desolately. 'That quack Krankenschwindler reckons this right leg could take longer to needle up the knitwear than the left one did.'

'Tough Gorgonzola,' said Blotto sympathetically.

Crocker let out an ironic little laugh. 'Have to be Chäs Luzvimmen out here,' he said. 'No other cheeses allowed to clock into the club.'

Blotto looked vacant. This required no effort at all on his part.

'Actually, Blotters me old treasury note,' his friend went on, 'there's a bit of a favourette I'd like to float past your barge . . .'

'Good ticket,' said Blotto. 'Any quid-pro I can do for a fellow muffin-toaster . . . no skin off my rice pudding. So, come on, what is it? Uncage the ferrets.'

'Talking of muffin-toasters . . .'

'Yes?'

'. . . you know Victor Muke-Wallingborough?'

'Lewdie? Of course I do. Is the King German?'

'Well, Lewdie's done a bit of backdoor-sidling.'

'Has he, by Denzil? The four-faced filcher! He's sold you up the river for a handful of winkle shells?'

'Not to put too fine a point on it, that's exactly what he's done.'

'The oikish sponge-worm! Boddoes from Eton don't do that to other boddoes from Eton.'

'No, they don't.'

'We have our standards. So, what did the out-of-bounder do to you, Crocker?'

'He said that I wasn't a sportsman.'

So devastating was this statement to Blotto that he couldn't prevent himself from saying, 'Broken biscuits!' And even that wasn't strong enough to express the level of affront he felt. He followed up with 'Biscuits broken in a hundred million pieces!'

Crocker was too shocked to reply for a moment. He'd seen Blotto in moments of stress before, usually towards the end of cricket matches, but never witnessed his old muffin-toaster lose control so totally.

'What exactly did the bucket of bilge-water say to you?' asked Blotto, recovering himself. 'The exact words?'

'Lewdie said . . .' Crocker spoke slowly, fearful that he too might lose control. 'He said that the reason I was always getting injured was because I was afraid of sport. I got injured deliberately to get out of playing.'

Blotto's mouth goldfished for some moments.

Finally, the silence was broken by his injured friend. 'Obviously, behaviour like that demands revenge . . .'

Blotto had recovered sufficiently to utter a confirmatory, 'Is a cricket ball round?'

'. . . and I'm too crocked up here to do much about it in the short term . . .'

Blotto was ahead of him. When it came to matters of honour, he always knew where his duty lay. 'Don't don your worry-boots about it, Crocker me old ebony cigarette holder. If I don't see the proper revenge is exacted, then you can call me a ratcatcher's bait!'

'I knew I could rely on you, Blotters. You always were a Grade A foundation stone.'

Blotto blushed modestly. Compliments never failed to bring him out in crimps.

'And,' Crocker continued, 'if the revenge can have something to do with that slugbucket Lewdie's precious Croissant Run, then that would all be creamy éclair.'

'Leave it with me,' said Blotto firmly. 'The word of a Lyminster never wavers, even in a spoffing hurricane!'

The siblings breakfasted together the following morning, but Twinks did not mention the contents of the letter she had received at Schloss Luzvimmen. Nor did she tell her brother her plans for the day.

Blotto, secure in the knowledge that there were plenty of his old muffin-toasters around to spend time with – and, more importantly, one on whom revenge must be wreaked – did not ask about his sister's intentions. He just continued to moan about the holes in the cheese.

Back in her bedroom, Twinks checked the contents of her sequined reticule and added a few more essentials. She dressed warmly in white fur, so that she would not stand out in the snowy landscape, and put on stout boots, also white. Her approach to the Convent of the Sacred Icicle would not be heralded by the arrival of a horse-drawn sleigh. She would be working under cover, virtually melting into the snowy landscape.

When all was ready, she slipped unnoticed out of a back door of the Hotel Luzvimmen.

* * *

Count von Strapp had summoned Ulrich Weissfeder to the Schloss for an update on the English visitors.

Unlike most of the people who worked for him, the hotel manager was allowed inside one of the secret labs, where he found his boss experimenting with something that looked very like cheese. But it was not the creamy Chäs Luzvimmen with holes in it. Though their colour was the same, what von Strapp had in a Petri dish were firm little pellets about the size of rabbit droppings.

When Weissfeder's sharp knock on the door had been greeted with permission to enter, the Count looked up from his desk and said, 'Would you like to see the new invention that is going to cause revolutions in the whole of Europe, probably the whole of the world?'

The hotel manager, so rarely granted any insight into his employer's experimentation, said that indeed he would.

'Then watch.'

Also on the desk was a two-litre beer glass with about half an inch of colourless fluid at the bottom. With great precision, the Count took a pair of tweezers, picked up one of the pellets from the Petri dish and dropped it into the beer glass.

There was a slight fizzing sound, then the small ball suddenly expanded. Within seconds, the glass was full and excess cheese was spilling down over its sides. Nanoseconds later, it had solidified into an impermeable shell.

Count von Strapp turned to his underling, anticipating the compliment, which duly came. 'Eure Exzellenz, that is brilliant! With one masterstroke you have solved the problem of spreading Chäs Luzvimmen around the world. The transportation costs of these cheese pellets will save you millions of francs.'

The Count smiled with satisfaction. He had felt slightly rash after revealing his new creation to Weissfeder, but he'd been so excited that he had to demonstrate it to someone. And if the hotel manager thought the only purpose of the expanding cheese was to save transport costs, then no harm was done. The more sinister applications of his invention would remain secret. So would the revolutionary fact that he had finally developed a cheese with no holes in it. The visitor to the laboratory was totally unaware of the consequences of that breakthrough. Which, from the Count's point of view, was exactly the required outcome.

'The reason I called you here, Weissfeder, was concerning your two new English guests at the hotel.'

'Of course, Eure Exzellenz.'

'As you know, last night I entertained them here at the Schloss.'

'Yes, Eure Exzellenz.'

'And I couldn't decide what the two of them were doing here in Luzvimmen.'

'Their avowed purpose, as I mentioned before, is to find the sister of one of Lady Honoria's friends.'

'Yes, yes, I know that,' said the Count dismissively. 'But I think that is just a smokescreen. I am interested in the real purpose of their visit.'

'I told you they are spies, Eure Exzellenz.'

'Yes, spies working for the one whose name is not to be spoken.' An involuntary shudder ran through the Count's eyebrows at the reminder of his potential nemesis. 'Are we sure that is who are they spying for? What information are they hoping to find?'

'I will use all the resources at my command to find the answers to those questions, Eure Exzellenz.'

'I wonder whether it is worth your trouble,' said the Count.

'Oh?' Ulrich Weissfeder was surprised by his boss's apparent casualness.

'They are clearly spies, and as such – regardless of who they are spying for – they should be eliminated.'

The hotel manager understood exactly what his superior meant. There was no need for further explanation. 'Very good, Eure Exzellenz.'

'Hmm . . .' The Count mused. 'The woman has clearly got an exceptional brain . . .'

'Undoubtedly.'

'. . . but I wouldn't be surprised if the brother turned out to be the mastermind for their operation.'

Ulrich Weissfeder was taken aback. 'What on earth makes you think that, Eure Exzellenz?'

'Just that . . . nobody could really be as stupid as he appears to be.'

'I can assure you, Eure Exzellenz, having spent time with the young man at Tawcester Towers in England, he is exactly as stupid as he appears to be. If not stupider.'

'Ah. I wouldn't have thought that was possible.'

'Many strange phenomena are to be found in the ranks of the English aristocracy.'

'I have heard that.'

'Very few chins, though.'

'Hm.' The Count touched his hands together, as if finishing with the subject. 'Anyway, I'll hand over disposing of him to you, Weissfeder. Usual thing . . . make it look like a fatal accident.'

'Of course, Eure Exzellenz.'

'It is fortunate that winter sports offer so many opportunities for fatal accidents.'

'It is indeed, Eure Exzellenz. And – would you believe ...' He smiled an evil smile. '... the young man has already shown an interest in the Croissant Run ...'

'Then your path is clear.' The Count chuckled. Ulrich Weissfeder, privileged by complicity, joined in.

'What about the girl?' he asked. 'I don't think she has shown much interest in winter sports, but there are other ways. Do you require me to organise her elimination too?'

'Don't worry,' said Count von Strapp, recalling with a smile the contents of the envelope which had been given to Twinks. 'I have already arranged that.'

9

Twinks Investigates

Twinks was not to know that the route provided in the mysterious envelope would take her somewhere her brother had been that very day. A map gave directions to the cellar under the sanatorium where Crocker Wilmslow was laid up. Cellars were important parts of Luzvimmen properties, home to cattle during the winter, as in Schloss Luzvimmen and Heidi's parents' house. The sanatorium's cellar led to the one under the main convent, a storeroom which was also home to a laundry for the large amount of linen needed in such a place.

There was a noticeboard attached to one wall, with various pieces of paper pinned to it. Some were details of cleaning rotas, but there was one which Twinks deduced listed the arrivals and departures of finishing school pupils. In vain she looked for evidence that Aurelia ffrench-Windeau had left the premises. No, according to the listings, she was still in the building. Twinks used her photographic memory to record other information on the sheet.

What the cellar also contained, though – and the information had been in the envelope from Schloss

Luzvimmen – was a wardrobe of spare habits and finishing school uniforms used by the nuns and schoolgirls who lived in the Convent of the Sacred Icicle.

As instructed by her unknown guide, Twinks sought out a nun's habit that was the right size for her. Also, covering all bases, she took one of the school uniforms and stowed it in her sequined reticule. She left her own white garments at the bottom of a wardrobe, to be changed back into when she departed. Thus, to any uninformed witness who happened to see her, Lady Honoria Lyminster became a nun. Even with perfect hair covered and the slender outline of her body obscured by the black habit, she still managed to look sensational. Whatever her circumstances, Twinks was incapable of looking drab.

She was unobserved while she made the change. Indeed, she didn't see anyone inside either of the cellars.

From the second one, a passageway led off, presumably into the main part of the Convent of the Sacred Icicle. It was so dark in there that Twinks had to use the electric torch which she always kept in her sequined reticule. Its beam revealed a drapery of cobwebs, and Twinks's sensible nun's sandals crunched on the gritty floor, suggesting that the tunnel had not been used for some time. That suited her well, reducing the chances of her running into anyone.

Sensing an obstacle ahead, Twinks raised her torch beam. An old door, furry with the dust of ages, blocked her way. Its keyhole was huge. Twinks reached into her sequined reticule for the relevant picklocks, but stopped when she noticed that the dust around the keyhole had been wiped away. She tried the handle. The door gave under the slightest pressure. Maybe, whoever had sorted out the maps and other contents of the Schloss Luzvimmen envelope had prepared the way, making sure she had unimpeded access to the Convent of the Sacred Icicle.

Alternatively, maybe that person was guiding her into a trap.

There was a quotation buzzing round like a trapped bee in the vacancy of Blotto's brain. This was unusual. Though the beaks at Eton had been quite hot on quotations (many in Latin or Greek), few of the *bons mots* had exercised any purchase on the slippery surface of his memory. There was something he vaguely remembered by some boddo that began, 'To be or not to be . . .', but he couldn't recall the rest of the sentence.

The quotation troubling him that morning, however, was different. It was Crocker's mention of revenge that had set his mind whirring. 'Revenge is a . . .' 'Revenge is a . . . ?' 'Revenge is a . . . ?' 'Revenge is a fish!' Yes, he was getting somewhere. He really concentrated – and it came to him.

'Revenge is a fish best served hot.' He'd got there. Blotto felt the rare sensation of having met and triumphed over an intellectual challenge.

But getting the quotation right didn't advance him much further in deciding what form his revenge on Victor Muke-Wallingborough should take. Even though it was a proxy revenge on behalf of Buffy 'Crocker' Wilmslow, it was not a matter to be taken lightly. And traditional old school revenges, like holding Lewdie's head down in the toilet bowl while flushing it, just wouldn't be the right length of banana for the current circumstances.

The revenge had to be commensurate with the offence, that was the important thing. And it was hard to think of a worse offence than accusing a boddo – an Old Etonian muffin-toaster, at that – of deliberately getting injured to avoid playing sport.

Blotto racked his brain. As usual, there wasn't much to rack.

The ancient door opened on to an unexpected scene. Because she had come through a tunnel from the cellars, Twinks had assumed that she would emerge at ground level of the space beneath the Convent of the Sacred Icicle. But, to her surprise, she found herself in a high gallery, looking down on a chapel-like area beneath.

Fortunately, the door had opened silently, not with the creaks that might have been expected from a structure of that vintage. Again, Twinks wondered whether whoever had produced the guidelines for her had oiled the hinges to ease her passage.

As she entered the chapel, nuns were singing in a language that she did not recognise. This was almost unheard of. Twinks knew all of the world's languages and was fluent in most of them. The hymn – or incantation – came to an end, and she felt acute frustration that she hadn't understood a word of it.

From her vantage point, she had a perfect view of what was happening below. A circle of nuns stood with their backs to her. Near the altar, she recognised the bent back view of Sister Benedicta. Twinks could not see any of their faces or wimples, so all was black. Facing them stood Sam, the Mother Superior. In the surrounding darkness, an ethereal light seemed to emanate from her face.

But the greater colour contrast came from the diminutive figure who stood beside Sister Anneliese-Marie. A young girl, dressed in a nun's habit and wimple of gleaming white.

The face, which was almost as colourless, belonged unmistakably to Aurelia ffrench-Windeau.

Before Blotto did anything else, he went down to the stable where the Lagonda was stored. And there, unsurprisingly, he found Corky Froggett, trying to defend the magnificent bodywork from the depredations of frost. By cleaning and polishing, of course.

'Good morning, milord,' said the chauffeur, standing firmly at attention and touching his cap in salute. 'I trust you are having an enjoyable time in Switzerland.'

It wasn't the moment to share his woes about how to fulfil the charge he'd been given by Crocker, or indeed get on to the subject of the holes in the cheese, so Blotto just replied, 'All tickey-tockey. But how about you, Corky? You must be as bored as a twelve-bore outside the shooting season.'

The chauffeur, who had just received the ministrations of Heidi in the hayloft, asserted that he was managing to keep himself busy. 'And Lady Honoria, milord? I hope she is also enjoying her alpine sojourn?'

Blotto, still miffed that his sister hadn't confided her plans for the day to him, replied, a little testily, 'I assume so. No skin off my rice pudding if she isn't.'

'Very good, milord,' said the chauffeur, recognising when a subject had been ended. 'Is there anything I can do for you, milord? Drive you anywhere?' he added hopefully.

'No thanks, Corkers. These horse-drawn sleighs seem to fit the pigeon-hole round here.'

'Very good, milord,' said a disappointed Corky Froggett.

'Just a wodjermabit I need to extract from the dickey and I'll pongle off.'

'Very good, milord.' Over many years of his employment at Tawcester Towers, the chauffeur had got used to producing that formula of words when he was feeling the exact opposite.

Blotto took what he needed and availed himself of one of the Hotel Luzvimmen horse-drawn sleighs to take him back down to the Croissant Run clubroom. Revenge, he thought moodily – apart from being 'a fish best served hot' – was a fumaciously tricky business. It wasn't so difficult when real criminals were involved. The time-honoured principle of 'an eye for an eye, a tooth for a tooth, a swindle for a swindle, a murder for a murder' worked pretty well in those circs.

But when it was revenge on one of one's own muffin-toasters . . . not so easy.

The revenge still had to match the crime, though. And the nature of Victor Muke-Wallingborough's offence against Buffy 'Crocker' Wilmslow hiked up the hazard. Crocker had effectively been accused of cowardice, one of the worst charges that one Old Etonian could level against another. But how could anyone – let alone Blotto – find a plausible way of accusing Victor Muke-Wallingborough of cowardice?

Lewdie was, after all, acknowledged to be the bravest person in any room. An impartial observer might have qualified that by saying Lewdie was the bravest man in any room that didn't contain Devereux Lyminster, but Blotto himself was far too modest to support such an assertion. It didn't do for a boddo to run up the flag about himself. Such behaviour was the province of oikish sponge-worms like grammar school boys and solicitors.

As he entered the Croissant Run clubroom, he realised he was no nearer knowing how to exact Crocker's revenge.

Surely an accusation of cowardice could only be matched by another accusation of cowardice.

Yes, a tough rusk to chew.

Fortunately for Twinks, the language the Mother Superior spoke in her prayers was traditional Swiss German, not the unrecognisable babel tongue that the assembled nuns had been singing.

'We are gathered here,' Sister Anneliese-Marie intoned, 'within the Convent of the Sacred Icicle, in the Chapel of the Secret Order, for a solemn ceremony of induction.

'Few novices are worthy of entry to the Secret Order. All in this building, of course, are pure of thought and mind, but some have, above and beyond such virtues, a quality which can only be described as saintliness.'

Rein in the roans a moment there, thought Twinks. Surely you're not talking about Aurelia ffrench-Windeau? The despair of governesses, schoolteachers, and all other representatives of authority? The 'Devil of the Dorms'?

'It is rare,' the Mother Superior went on, 'that we encounter such a postulant. Rarer still that the person in question is not of Swiss nationality. And rare almost to the point of unbelievability that she should come from England, that land of lethargy and lackadaisical religion.'

Twinks bristled at this insult to the Land of the Golden Lions, but she knew it wasn't the moment to remonstrate. She listened as Sister Anneliese-Marie continued, 'So, today, we welcome into the Secret Order, the Order whose name can never be mentioned, a young woman who, while not yet a Bride of Christ, is at least engaged to him. I refer, of course, to the young woman by my side, whose name, now and for ever, will be Sister Liselotte.'

The name was greeted by a communal indrawn breath from the assembled nuns.

'Yes, I know why you react that way. The name "Liselotte" is not one that is given lightly in the Convent of the Sacred Icicle. It is the name, as you all know, of the saint to whom this foundation is dedicated. For that reason, it has never before been given to a postulant, either in our Order or in the Secret Order.

'Which may be a measure of the sanctity of the person who is being admitted into the Secret Order today.'

We can't still be talking about Aurelia, can we? thought Twinks.

'And now,' the Mother Superior announced, 'before we leave Sister Liselotte to the Solitary Reflection which is so much a part of her induction into the Secret Order, we will sing the Hymn of Acceptance. This confirms the admission of a new postulant into the Secret Order. It is an ancient, much-hallowed text, and its singing takes on the significance of a sacrament. The arcane language exerts a miraculous power that provides a direct link between the postulant and all three Members of the Trinity.'

On a hand cue from their Mother Superior, the nuns began the hymn. There was some uncertainty in their approach, explained presumably by the fact that it was a work they very rarely had to perform. But somehow this didn't matter. It was more of an incantation or spell than a hymn, anyway. Once again, frustratingly for Twinks, it was in a language she couldn't understand. Probably the same one that had featured earlier.

'We will now,' Sister Anneliese-Marie intoned solemnly at the end of the hymn, 'leave Sister Liselotte to her Solitary Reflection. Let silence reign throughout the Chapel of the Secret Order!'

102

This was the cue for the circle of nuns to back away from the white figure of Sister Liselotte, almost as if she was suffering from some infectious disease.

But it was also the cue for a moment of drama. Sister Benedicta, whose role it clearly was to stage such special effects, pulled a lever. Immediately the wooden panels behind the altar slid to the sides, revealing the sheer face of the glacier of which Twinks had seen part on the floor above. There was less natural light down at this level, but again she could perceive the blurred outlines of human figures immobilised in the ice. Three this time. So, she thought, there are at least five Phantom Skiers, should their services in protecting the Convent of the Sacred Icicle ever be called upon.

The revelation of the glacier behind the altar was an anticipated cue for the assembled nuns. Led by their Mother Superior, they filed out of the chapel. Sister Benedicta brought up the rear. The door to the rest of the convent was closed with a booming report, followed by the rattle and creaks of various locks and bars being secured.

Sister Liselotte – or Aurelia ffrench-Windeau – appeared not to be aware of the nuns' departure. The moment the glacier had been revealed, she had turned towards it, transfixed. Or perhaps she was turning towards the cross in front, the one part of the altar which had stayed in place when the great doors opened.

Having had her attention drawn to it, Twinks realised something unusual about the cross. Both the upright and the crossbeam were made of skis.

Blotto entered the Croissant Run clubroom to sounds of wild rejoicing. He didn't find this odd. His Old Etonian muffin-toasters were always a rowdy lot. But the level of raucousness really was remarkable. It must have been something unusual that they were celebrating.

He soon saw the cause of the excessive uproar. Victor Muke-Wallingborough was standing by the blackboard watching with relish as the scorer rubbed out Blotto's 1 minute 17.31 seconds and chalked in Lewdie's recent 1 minute 15.07 seconds.

The new hero was surrounded by congratulating muffin-toasters.

'Beezer time on the 'boggan!' cried one.

'Nice innings, Lewdie!' cried another.

'You really are the panda's panties!'

'You're made of pure brick-mix, Lewdie!'

'You're a Grade A foundation stone!'

'And fancy doing the Croissant Run with only one hand on the 'boggan!'

Victor Muke-Wallingborough responded to this last remark. 'Well, the whole clangdumble was getting as easy as a one-bush maze. So, I thought I'd raise the stakes, hike up the hazard a bit.'

There was a smoothness, almost an insolence about the way he said this. And, as he did so, he looked directly at Blotto.

Though slow of understanding in some areas of life, Devereux Lyminster didn't need any explanations when it came to rivalry with another muffin-toaster. Latin, Greek and mathematics may have slipped through the colander of his brain, but he fully got the message when someone was challenging him.

Broken biscuits, he thought wretchedly. This was not because he didn't think he could meet the challenge. Improving on Lewdie's time on the Croissant Run – and doing it with only one hand on the 'boggan . . . that would be as easy as a housemaid's virtue.

But finding a reason to accuse Victor Muke-Wallingborough of cowardice in the new circumstances . . .

That would be as tough as a rhino's rump.

Sister Liselotte remained frozen in position, looking at the cross of skis, as Twinks approached her.

'Aurelia,' the visitor said. It was the name she preferred.

The girl turned to face her. 'I'm sorry. I do not think I recognise you, Sister.'

'I'm not a Sister!' said Twinks heartily. 'I'm Twinks. Berry's friend. And I've come to get you out of this horracious treacle tin. Come on, don't fiddle round the fir trees. Come with me, and we'll be out of this gluepot as quick as two ferrets in a rabbit warren.'

'But I can't come with you,' said the white-clad postulant.

'Why not, in the name of Viscount Melbourne?'

'Because,' said Sister Liselotte, 'I have a vocation.'

10

Is Twinks Finished?

Twinks's plans to argue further with the recalcitrant postulant were interrupted by the sounds of keys in locks and metal bars being moved on the other side of the door through which the nuns had just exited. She rushed back up the stairs to the gallery and was safely out of sight by the time a suspicious-looking Sister Benedicta re-entered the chapel.

Aurelia ffrench-Windeau showed no signs of having seen the new arrival. Her focus did not shift from the crossed skis in front of her. Sister Benedicta busied herself with collecting up hymn books and putting them in neat piles, but Twinks could tell this was only being done to give the elderly nun the appearance of busyness. She was really there to keep an eye on the new Sister Liselotte.

This gave Twinks hope. If Sister Benedicta thought it was necessary to keep an eye on the girl, that could well mean that Aurelia's penchant for mischief had not been completely subdued by her vocation. Surely the appalling threat of being seen as a 'GLG' would temper her behaviour?

Twinks, meanwhile, got on with what she had to do. This was Plan B, which had not been contained in the instructions envelope, but which she had worked out in the storeroom while she'd been changing into the nun's habit.

Plan B involved a different disguise. She withdrew the finishing schoolgirl's costume from her sequined reticule and deftly changed from the nun's habit into it. She reached again into the ever-rewarding sequined reticule and took out some make-over essentials.

She did not use her electric torch, for fear of alerting Sister Benedicta down in the chapel, but she was sufficiently practised to manage her transformation in the dark. She knew, because they had been mentioned so often by amorous swains, that her distinguishing features above the neck were her beautiful eyes, her beautiful skin and her beautiful hair. Disguise those and nobody would recognise her.

The azure eyes were easily obscured by thick glasses, with lenses like the bottom of jam jars and tortoiseshell frames. Judicious application of make-up turned the alabaster of her skin to something more sallow, spotty and adolescent. (So upmarket was the quality of her make-up supplier that the adolescent spots were actually squeezable.) And the glory of her ash-blonde hair was effectively covered by a straw-coloured wig with plaits. Somehow, as she walked down the stairs into the chapel, she had managed to lose a decade and develop the recalcitrant shuffle of a thirteen-year-old-girl.

Sister Benedicta turned at the sound of her descending footsteps.

'Who are you?' she demanded in her rough Swiss German. 'What are you doing here?'

Twinks was glad of the attention she'd paid to the list in the storeroom of the finishing school's pupils' comings and goings. 'My name is Sylviane Heffelfinger,' she said in perfect – if adolescently squeaky – Swiss German. 'Today is the day I am meant to be joining the finishing school of the Convent of the Sacred Icicle. But I am afraid I have lost my way in this building with which I am not familiar.'

Her research was accurate. Sister Benedicta conceded that they were expecting a new pupil called Sylviane Heffelfinger to join the finishing school. 'But you are meant to be arriving the day after tomorrow.'

'The plans of my parents changed,' said the new pupil. 'It was more convenient for them to bring me here today.'

'Very well,' said the old nun grudgingly. 'I will take you where you are meant to be. Though how you managed to get into this part of the building, I cannot begin to imagine.'

'I do not have a good sense of direction,' Sylviane Heffelfinger apologised.

As she was led away by Sister Benedicta, Twinks tried to make eye contact with the newly inducted Sister Liselotte.

She failed. There was no reaction from the girl. No interest.

Her eyes maintained their fixed gaze on the cross of skis.

The finishing school and its accommodation were on the first floor of the Convent of the Sacred Icicle, separate from the nuns' cells, refectory and other offices. Apart from a few major dates in the church calendar when the girls joined the community in the large ground-floor chapel, they saw little of the sisters, except for the ones who actually taught them.

Of these, the most important was Sister Dagmar, a tall, unsmiling woman who appeared resentful of the fact that she had been born. It was to Sister Dagmar that Sister Benedicta handed over her charge, before departing, maybe back to her spying on the new initiate of the Secret Order, Sister Liselotte.

'You call me Sister,' said the teacher to the transformed Twinks. 'I call you Sylviane. All girls in the school are addressed by their Christian names.'

Sylviane Heffelfinger was taken through to the school's dormitories and shown the bed allocated to her. The conditions were less Spartan than English girls' boarding schools that Twinks's friends had described to her. She, of course, had been educated at Tawcester Towers by a series of governesses, who had to be quickly replaced as their intellects were outstripped by their pupil's, so she had never been in a dormitory.

But, except for the fact that she would be sharing it with eleven other girls, there was no cause for complaint. The large room was clean, spacious and warm.

'Where is your luggage?' asked Sister Dagmar. 'Your belongings?'

'My parents,' said Twinks, thinking on her feet, 'changed the tick-tock on my arrival here but failed to do the same on the arrival of my spoffing trunk. That'll be pongling over here the day after tomorrow.'

(Needless to say, her command of colloquial Swiss German was such that she found the exact equivalent words for 'tick-tock', 'spoffing' and 'pongling'.)

'Very well,' said a grudging Sister Dagmar. 'If there's anything you need, you'll have to borrow from one of the other girls.'

'Splendissimo!' said Twinks. (Because of the proximity to the Italian border, this worked in both languages.)

'And, incidentally, Sylviane,' said Sister Dagmar, 'one thing you should know . . . We don't approve of the use of slang in the Convent of the Sacred Icicle.'

'Tickey-tockey,' said the new pupil. 'Good ticket.'

The look the teaching nun turned on her charge was sourer than a bottle of Château d'Yquem that had been uncorked for a fortnight. 'Right,' she said. 'Your behaviour clearly needs a lot of work done on it. I will take you down to the classroom, where you will start the process of becoming a finished young lady.'

It has to be said that Twinks did find the finishing school curriculum pretty sterile. She was glad her participation in the system was to be of short duration.

It goes without saying that the pupils at the Convent of the Sacred Icicle were not taught anything actually useful. Proficiency in cookery, dressmaking or other domestic skills would not be required in the world for which they were being prepared. Indeed, ability in any of those areas would mark them out as 'the wrong sort of person'. In the lives they aspired to, there would be servants to deal with all that gubbins.

The main objection Twinks had to what was being taught was that she knew it all. Of course, she knew everything, but correct social behaviour was something that had been infused into her with her bottles of baby milk (not, of course, her mother's milk – the Dowager Duchess didn't do that kind of thing).

So, learning deportment by walking round the classroom with a hymn book balanced on her head was completely unnecessary for Twinks. She had always carried herself perfectly. Learning which cutlery to use at a banquet was also something she just instinctively knew. And the one lesson she underwent on conversation in social situations caused considerable biting of her lip. The instinct to remonstrate was almost overwhelming.

It wasn't the advice on the etiquette of conversation taught by the nuns that offended her. It was the content. There were so many subjects that the finishing school pupils were taught to avoid. Politics, religion, literature; anything in fact that might suggest the speaker was in possession of more than one brain cell.

The fear that drove these prohibitions was the fear of frightening men. Frightening men off. Intelligence in a woman was a pretty scary phenomenon to be encountered by the average upper-class English male. The aim of finishing schools was to eradicate any trace of it in their potential spouses.

This approach to education made Twinks seethe. It made her seethe even more because this was not the first time she had encountered it. Growing up at Tawcester Towers, she had found that the Dowager Duchess shared some of these views. Twinks was constantly being encouraged to dampen down her intellect in masculine company. And her failure to have secured a husband was frequently attributed to her unwillingness to follow her mother's advice on this matter.

Not that Twinks herself was worried about her unmarried state. The transactions she had witnessed between her parents had not proved to be much of an advertisement for the institution. The principle of seeing as little of each other as possible was not, to her mind, a good basis for an enduring relationship.

Twinks had not ruled out the prospect of getting married. But, like everything else in her life, it would have to be on her own terms. Those terms did not include disguising the person that she was, and certainly not pretending to be any less intelligent. Any man whom she accepted would, in his turn, have to accept – and, ideally, match – her level of intellect. Though amorous swains fell for her with the regularity of guardsmen in a heatwave, it was perhaps no surprise that she had yet to find her lifetime's partner.

So, as she went through the charade of being educated, or 'finished', she had to keep telling herself that the subterfuge would only be for a short time. And that her main purpose remained somehow to get Aurelia ffrench-Windeau out of the Convent of the Sacred Icicle.

She wasn't impressed by her fellow pupils, either. Most of them were of English extraction and, sadly, not her sort of people. Her attitude to them might be interpreted by some as snobbery, but to Lady Honoria Lyminster it was just the way things were. There were a few who had as much claim to the upper classes as Aurelia ffrench-Windeau, and none who approached Twinks's own status by the longest chalk stream in the kingdom.

She supposed there was some kind of necessity for such people to exist, though she couldn't, offhand, think what it might be. She just had no desire to spend time with them. What could she possibly have in common with the daughters of railway barons, newspaper barons, textile manufacturers, armament manufacturers, American parvenus and solicitors?

They all did need finishing. Twinks didn't. She had been born the finished article.

* * *

It was obvious what Blotto had to do. The business of exacting Crocker's revenge on Victor Muke-Wallingborough must be put on hold. After what Lewdie had just done on the Croissant Run, there was no chance of making any accusation of cowardice against him in the immediate future.

More important was for Blotto to beat his rival's new record time. And to do it only holding on to the 'boggan with one hand.

'Lewdie, me old cycle clip, tickey-tockey if I have another pop at the partridge on the Croissant Run . . . ?'

'Of course, Blotto me old shaving brush holder. We've been holding the slot for you. We know how little you like coming second at anything.'

This was said with some edge, but Blotto, experienced in competitive sporting banter, didn't rise to it. Anyway, he was distracted by the appearance of someone he hadn't expected to see amongst his Old Etonian muffin-toasters. Moving without making eye contact with anyone, Ulrich Weissfeder sidled his way from the entrance to the run to the clubroom's main exit. Other people seeing him might have wondered what he was doing there, but Blotto never did much of that wondering stuff.

'Well, don't let's shimmy round the shrubbery,' said Blotto. 'Time I tootled over to the 'boggan, wouldn't you say, Lewdie?'

'Certainly would, Blotters.'

'And hold the flipmadoodle with one hand – is that the to-do?'

'Bong on the nose, Blotters. If you want to match my record, like for like.'

'Match it, Lewdie? Oh yes, and I'm an Apache dancer! I'm going to coffinate it!'

* * *

As she dragged herself through the tedium of the finishing school day, Twinks didn't pay much attention to her fellow pupils. Her brilliant mind was focused on the challenge of getting Aurelia ffrench-Windeau out of the Convent of the Sacred Icicle. The ideas weren't coming with their customary fluency, but at least she was inside the building.

She didn't for a moment believe the authenticity of Aurelia's vocation. The girl must have been threatened or bullied or blackmailed to go through the initiation process Twinks had witnessed. Being a 'GLG' was just not part of her make-up. Twinks felt certain that, given more time, she could easily persuade Aurelia of the advantages of escape.

But she'd have to move fast. The safety of her disguise as Sylviane Heffelfinger wouldn't last for ever. For one thing, the real Sylviane was due to appear soon. She'd have to get Aurelia out that night. Twinks hadn't yet conceived a plan as to how that goal would be achieved but, confident in the power of her mighty intellect, she knew she would have one by the time she needed it.

The last lesson ended, and the girls went to their dormitories to freshen up before their evening meal. The amount of expensive perfume that was sprayed or dabbed on bore witness to the wealth that their parents had accumulated by industry and trade. (Twinks, of course, knew that these were not proper ways of arriving at money. The only respectable means of acquisition of the old jingle-jangle was by inheriting it.)

She herself, the fictional luggage not having arrived, had no means of freshening up. But it couldn't have mattered less. Women of Twinks's beauty remain permanently fresh. Still, she was, of course, in disguise. So, she did some token squeezing of her artificial spots.

As the others departed for the refectory, there was a girl

who lingered in the dormitory. Twinks had identified her in the classroom as one of the few Swiss nationals in the group. And it was in Swiss German that the girl spoke when they were alone.

'I want to know what you're playing at,' she said, looking directly at the new arrival.

'Who are you?' asked Twinks, channelling the Dowager Duchess's *hauteur* very effectively into Swiss German.

'My name is Gretchen Kohlschuffler.'

'Oh?' The monosyllable was shorthand for: 'Why on earth should that be of interest to me?'

'And I am a friend of Sylviane Heffelfinger.'

'Ah.'

'So, I know that you are not Sylviane Heffelfinger.'

Lewdie and a lot of the other muffin-toasters gathered around the start of the Croissant Run. The one delegated to give the signal to the timekeeper down below had his finger ready on the red light switch. The air was heavy with raucous cries and Old Etonian indecencies.

Blotto lay face down on the 'boggan. He gripped the front rail with his right hand and, with his left, suddenly produced what he had brought from the Lagonda's dickey and concealed down his trouser leg. He waved it in Victor Muke-Wallingborough's direction.

'Thought it'd be creamy éclair to add another hazard, Lewdie,' he cried. And he treasured the sour look his words brought to his rival's patrician features.

Though he had only completed the run once, Blotto had learnt a lot from that experience. The secret to shaving seconds off the time of descent was shifting the body weight at significant points on the trajectory. Though the beaks at Eton had despaired of his arithmetical skills, he instinctively understood the mathematics of this kind of challenge.

Blotto gestured to the muffin-toasters holding the 'boggan that it was their cue to let go. The signal light was switched on as, brandishing his cricket bat with cheerful abandon, he let the accelerating descent begin.

It happened at the first sharp bend, the 'Widowmaker', which had ended Buffy 'Crocker' Wilmslow's last attempt.

Something in the side wall gave way.

Blotto and 'boggan together shot like a guided missile into the void, at the bottom of which lay the icy jagged crags of the Altzberg mountain.

11

The Secrets of the Cheese-Processing Works

Count von Strapp had been waiting for the signal. He'd had one of his telescopes trained on the doorway between the clubroom and the start of the Croissant Run for some time. When he saw Blotto emerge and take up his position on the 'boggan, he smiled in anticipation.

His smile grew broader as he saw that the young idiot was waving a cricket bat.

The red light came on. Blotto was launched down the frozen chute. Just at the point where it should have happened, the outside wall gave way. Man and 'boggan flew off into oblivion.

Count von Strapp didn't watch any more. He knew no one could survive the impact of a fall like that on the Altzberg. He went back to his desk to fine-tune his plans for imminent world domination.

And he congratulated himself on what a useful tool for his use he'd turned Ulrich Weissfeder into.

He just hoped his other hatchet men had found as effective a way of eliminating the sister.

* * *

'All right,' Twinks responded defiantly. 'You're bong on the nose that I'm not Sylviane Heffelfinger. Give that pony a rosette! But what's your to-do about it? Are you going to sell me down the plughole to the Mother Superior?'

'Not straight away,' Gretchen Kohlschuffler replied cautiously. 'First I want to know why you've come to the Convent of the Sacred Icicle in disguise?'

'Because I'm trying to find a poor droplet who's the sister of one of my chumbos.' There were times, Twinks knew, when the truth could prove at least as effective as any subterfuge.

'What's the poor droplet's name?'

'Aurelia ffrench-Windeau.'

'Ah. She is a strange one.'

'Sorry, not on the same bus. Why do you say "strange"?'

'Aurelia is strange because, just in the short time she has been here, she has changed completely.'

'What does that mean when it's got its spats on? Come on, uncage the ferrets.'

'When Aurelia arrived here,' Gretchen explained, 'she was the worst-behaved girl in the school. She didn't do any work and she broke all the rules. She was rude to the nuns, she smuggled alcohol and cigarettes into the dormitory, and she kept trying to escape so that she could meet up with goat boys from the village.'

Twinks liked the sound of this. She recognised Berengaria's sister, the Aurelia ffrench-Windeau she had known and loved, the Devil of the Dorms. The one who would never be a 'Good Little Girl'. 'So, what made the poor little thimble change?'

Gretchen's brow furrowed in frustration. 'I really don't know, but I'm sure the Mother Superior was behind it. Suddenly, Aurelia became very pious. I used to try to sit beside her in the back row during lessons. Guaranteed to have a good snigger together ... and often a good few swigs of Pflümfli, Träsch, Williamine or Kirsch.' (Needless to say, Twinks recognised all these names of Swiss liqueurs.)

'And when did this spoffing change happen?'

'Within the last week. First, Aurelia became very pious. Then, a couple of days ago, she disappeared. She's done that many times and usually all the nuns start questioning us as to where she might have gone and which goat boy she's been in touch with recently. This time, nothing. Which makes me think the Mother Superior knows exactly where she is – and may well have put her there.'

Twinks nodded thoughtfully. 'I think you could have popped the partridge bong on the nose.'

'What do you mean?' asked Gretchen. 'Do you know where Aurelia is? Have you seen her?'

Twinks was silent for a moment, then said, 'I have a little stratagemette. Would you agree to us knitting our noddles together on this?'

'Sorry? Not with you.'

'I'm prepared to share my gin-gen about Aurelia with you, if you agree to give me a jockey-up on getting her out of this fumacious place. Might that be the right length of banana for you?'

Gretchen Kohlschuffler's eyes gleamed with enthusiasm as she replied, 'I can't think of anything I'd enjoy more. When do we start?'

Having absolutely no imagination was sometimes a blessing for Blotto. Certainly, it was in moments of severe jeopardy. With the barometer of his mood set firmly to

119

'Sunny', his first conviction was always that, whatever the odds, he would survive. It was just a question of how that happy outcome should be achieved.

So, finding himself in freefall over a *cheval de frise* of icy, razor-sharp rocks did not cause him consternation. He had a track record of finding a way out of such gluepots. And this time his chances were even better because he had his cricket bat with him.

The first thing he'd done on shooting through the side wall of the Croissant Run was to release his hold on the toboggan which went flying off on its own trajectory. Then he transferred his cricket bat to his right hand and adjusted his body position. He moved from the horizontal into a diving posture, holding the cricket bat out in front of him. He knew that head injuries were more serious than leg injuries, but this orientation gave him more control over his descent.

He put his left hand on the bat too, shifting it around, so that the boat-shaped back of the willow would be first to touch ground. Now it was just a matter of steering himself so that he made landfall on frozen snow rather than jagged rock.

He judged it perfectly. The tip of the bat met the permafrost at the top of a narrow ravine and, acting like the prow of an icebreaker, slid him downwards at ferocious pace. As his body met the surface, the thick tweed (of his strong suit) only slightly slowed his progress.

Blotto realised that he would have more control if he was actually standing on the cricket bat. With difficulty, and still descending at a ridiculous speed, he managed to get himself upright on to the wooden surface. With one foot in front of the other, he found, by easing his body from side to side, he could control the trajectory.

120

From then on, it was a matter of gravity (as invented by either Sir Fig Newton or William Tell). And, as the steep mountainside gave way to the shallower gradients of the foothills, Blotto felt himself slowing down, until he came to a halt outside the yellow warehouses, which Twinks had observed and identified on their first arrival at Luzvimmen.

Blotto stepped from his cricket bat and brushed the accumulated snow and ice off his tweed suit (his strong one) and brogues.

He felt very satisfied with his recent escape.

He'd have felt even more satisfied had he realised that he'd invented the snowboard forty years ahead of anybody else. But, of course, he wasn't to know that.

He did, however, now know that the yellow warehouses by which he had ended up were part of the Chäs Luzvimmen cheese production business. He saw that all along one side of the largest building were a series of tall doors, as for a row of stables or possibly garages for motor vehicles. He remembered Count von Strapp saying that the buildings at the foot of the mountains were involved in the transportation of the cheese which flowed down the long tube from Schloss Luzvimmen.

One of the tall doors stood slightly ajar, so, since there seemed to be nobody about to observe his movements, Blotto slipped inside. The space was illuminated by working lights, and there was a powerful odour of . . . surprise, surprise . . . cheese.

Not stables, definitely garages, was his first thought. And very modern garages, at that. What was strangest about the sight that greeted him was the kind of vehicles the building housed. Of course, he knew nothing about the most efficient means of moving cheese from one place to another, but the heavy trucks he saw lined up did not in any way look like cheese carts.

He moved in for a closer inspection.

Twinks was relieved to have made the acquaintance and enlisted the support of Gretchen Kohlschuffler. Long experience of extricating herself from a variety of gluepots had taught her the value of input from someone with local knowledge. It was also encouraging that Gretchen seemed at least as keen as she was to find out what lay behind the transformation of Aurelia ffrench-Windeau.

The two finishing school pupils – or what appeared to be the two finishing school pupils – went down to join their classmates for the evening meal. They did not sit together. They did not want Sister Dagmar and her acolytes to have any suspicion of complicity between them. And they ate their very dull meal.

The food for the girls at the Convent of the Sacred Icicle was unfailingly dull. This was a concession to the fact that the preponderance of the pupils were English. The sole purpose of their education in Luzvimmen was to equip them for marriage. And, because the men at whom they were being targeted as marriage fodder had grown up through the culinary experiences of nursery food, public school food and gentlemen's club food, for them to feel at home, the menu had to be unfailingly dull.

From the conversation of her fellow pupils, it became clear to Twinks that she and Gretchen were not the only ones concerned by the absence of Aurelia ffrench-Windeau. It turned out that, in her short time at the finishing school, the Devil of the Dorms had built up an enviable reputation for the variety of services she provided for her schoolmates. Not only was she the source of all the bottles of Pflümfli, Träsch, Williamine and Kirsch which were smuggled into the Convent of the Sacred Icicle, she also provided a simple pimping operation, whereby she arranged assignations between her fellow pupils and Luzvimmen's goat boys. The curtailment – indeed, cessation – of these services was a cause of considerable frustration and annoyance. Unfinished business at the finishing school.

At the end of the meal, the two Aurelia-seeking conspirators lingered in the dining room. Trying to look as if she had something to do, for verisimilitude, Twinks squeezed an artificial spot.

Once Sister Dagmar's team was out of sight, with a finger to her lips, Gretchen led the way to a small anteroom where the food was passed from the kitchen before it was taken to the dining room.

'All right,' she whispered – in Swiss German, of course, 'you said you saw Aurelia in a chapel in the lowest part of the building?'

'Yes, but I'm not sure that I could retrace the way Sister Benedicta brought me back from there.' It was rare for Twinks to make such an admission of failure.

'Don't worry,' said Gretchen. 'I know the way.'

Twinks was surprised. 'Is it part of the prems where you biff the Bible bells too?'

'No. But ... well, Aurelia has used it as a place to arrange ... introductions to people ...'

Twinks was ahead of her. Armed with the new knowledge she'd gained during the meal, she asked, 'Do you mean "people" you might want to get under the same umbrella with?'

Gretchen blushed furiously. Twinks pressed on, 'People you might want to rumple the pump with?'

A very embarrassed 'Well . . .'

'Not to fiddle round the fir trees . . .' Twinks demanded, 'are you talking about rolling on camomile lawns with rampant goat boys?'

The expression – not to mention the colour – that spread over Gretchen Kohlschuffler's face told Twinks that she had pinged the right partridge.

'Then lead the way,' she said imperiously, 'to the scene of your debauches!'

Though the Lagonda was one of the Great Triptych of Loves in Blotto's life, the others being his cricket bat and his hunter Mephistopheles, he did not disregard other motor vehicles. His daily discussions with Corky Froggett about the beauties of the Lag's engineering invariably involved comparisons with lesser motors. And being, above all, a believer in fairness, Blotto didn't think you could properly disparage anything (except solicitors, obviously) without knowledge of the subject.

So, the eye he brought to the fleet of vehicles inside the Chäs Luzvimmen garages was an informed one. The first thing he noticed was that, like the exterior of the building, all of them were painted yellow. The second was that they didn't look as though they had been designed for the transport of food. Though that was not an area in which he had any specialised knowledge, Blotto was familiar with the lineaments of bakers' carts and butchers' carts. Indeed, his Lagonda, driving majestically down the centre of roads in Tawcestershire, had frequently forced such conveyances into the ditches on either side.

He was prepared to believe that the transport of cheese made special demands on vehicle designers. Particularly the transport of Swiss cheese, which made special demands on the credulity of the average man. (Blotto identified himself as 'the average man', an assessment which contrived to be at the same time very modest and very misguided. There was nothing average about his sporting prowess. Nor, at the other end of the scale, was there anything average about his intellect.)

For a start, there was that business about Swiss cheese having holes in it. That, to Blotto's mind, remained a total rum baba. Maybe the unstable constituency of such an offence against nature determined the way the cheese should be transported.

Then there was the way the cheese found its way down to the processing plants, in a long tube from the heights of Schloss Luzvimmen. Blotto wondered whether the long protuberances at the front of the vehicles attached to nozzles somewhere, and that was how their interior was loaded with cheese.

But he couldn't convince himself about that.

However much he tried to find other explanations for the metal tubes attached to the fronts of the yellow trucks, he came back to the fact that they looked like nothing so much as gun barrels.

And the amount of yellow armoured cladding on the trucks themselves made them look like nothing so much as tanks.

12

Mousetrapped!

Gretchen Kohlschuffler, with vivid memories of encounters with goat boys there, led the way easily back to the Chapel of the Secret Order. Following instructions to avoid the lower level, she entered the gallery from which the induction of Sister Liselotte had been witnessed. Twinks was delighted to see that the postulant, dressed in her glistening white habit, was still standing in front of the cross of skis. Because the day's light had gone, the glacier behind reflected only the glow of the few candles left in the chapel. The image was somehow gothic and spooky.

Remembering that her earlier approach to Aurelia ffrench-Windeau had been frustrated by talk of the girl's vocation, Twinks put a finger to her lips and gestured to Gretchen that she needed a moment to decide on their next move.

But events took over. The door that led from the Chapel of the Secret Order to the main convent opened to admit Sister Anneliese-Marie. Sister Liselotte turned to face the new arrival, in a manner suggesting she had been expecting her. The two nuns, one in black, one in white, stood facing each other. Then, on some unseen cue, both removed their habits.

The Mother Superior was now dressed exactly as on the first occasion Twinks had met her – white basque, white ankle-length bloomers and black boots. The removal of Aurelia's habit revealed a matching ensemble in black with white boots. Both retained their wimples, one black, one white.

Silently, they moved positions from facing each other to looking at the altar of crossed skis with the obscure sheen of the glacier behind.

Then Sister Anneliese-Marie announced, 'Let the devotions begin!'

Well-rehearsed, the two women moved in step towards the side panels of the Chapel of the Secret Order, which were painted with images of various nuns undergoing various martyrdoms. Together, their hands reached forward to grasp hidden handles. The panels turned out to be doors, which swung outwards.

Twinks could not believe what the Mother Superior and Sister Liselotte then pulled out of the storage space.

Down in the yellow buildings at the foot of the mountain, Blotto was continuing his tour of inspection. Every detail he encountered served to reinforce his impression that the main purpose of the fleet of vehicles there was not cheese transportation.

As he explored further, however, he did get into the cheesier area of the operation. Adjacent to the garages was a huge building where the long delivery tube from the manufacturing works in Schloss Luzvimmen ended up. The outlet, currently capped by a kind of lid, projected from high up on the wall, over three huge vats. Clearly it could be moved to fill whichever of them was emptiest. When Blotto checked, it seemed that all three vats were full. In each, huge paddles churned the warm goo, presumably to stop it from solidifying until it was ready to be poured into circular moulds and become rounds of Chäs Luzvimmen.

In a massive storeroom next door, the finished products were stacked up high on shelves. Some were still maturing, while others, with bands around them in the distinctive red and yellow livery of the brand, were ready for transportation to the biggest markets 'in the whole of Europe, probably the whole of the world'.

Continuing his progress through the interlinked buildings, Blotto found he was in another garage. This one housed new but traditional delivery lorries, which would obviously deliver Chäs Luzvimmen to the retail outlets, where it was destined to eclipse the sales of Appenzeller, Emmental, Sbrinz, and even Gruyère.

Having discovered this real, traditional method of cheese transportation, Blotto was even keener to find out the purpose of the vehicles garaged at the other end of the complex.

There was a noticeboard in the room where the vats were, which had lots of papers pinned to it. Thinking they might offer some clue to what was going on in the buildings, Blotto perused them.

Not much use because they were all in Swiss German. One had a picture of people skiing on it. Thinking it might be of interest if he could get it translated – in other words, when he next saw Twinks – Blotto stuffed it into his jacket pocket.

* * *

Twinks recognised what the Mother Superior and Sister Liselotte pulled out from behind the panels of the Chapel of the Secret Order. Two sets of boards on wheels.

They knew what to do with them. Moving the apparatus to the centre of the chapel, they took up parallel positions. On an unspoken signal, they both started shifting from side to side, controlling the boards by the strength of their thighs. They began slowly, but in perfect synchronicity, building up the pace of their movements until their supports were a flutter of perpetual motion. The two had clearly worked together before. No random pairing could ever have achieved the speed and mastery that they displayed.

And just at the moment Twinks was asking herself what, in the name of Viscount Melbourne, their actions had to do with religious devotions, Sister Anneliese-Marie started an incantation. Though it had the sound of a hymn or prayer, its words did not make any reference to God. They appeared to be a repetition, in various forms of words, of the plea, 'Make us stronger!' And the way the words were timed with the movements suggested that their rhythms were an essential part of the routine.

Twinks also noticed that, every now and then, the exercise changed. The pair of nuns shifted position, leaning, still with perfect choreography, either to the left side or the right. And the signal for these changes were the words from Sister Anneliese-Marie, 'We will defeat the Holy Temptation!'

For Twinks, who prided herself on her omniscience, not knowing what was going on was a source of fumacious frustration.

* * *

129

Though ineffective at tasks that called on brainpower or planning, Blotto was not without technical skills. His love for the Lagonda meant that he understood vehicles. His complicity with Mephistopheles had brought him a great aptitude for the management of horses. And as someone who had gone shooting every season since he'd been able to hold a gun (at the age of three), he did have an intuitive knowledge of weaponry.

He inspected the yellow tank-like vehicles and found one which was not locked. Still holding his cricket bat, he installed himself in the driver's seat. As well as the steering wheel, gear lever and dashboard essentials which he would have expected in any motorised conveyance, there was an array of other handles, switches and equipment which he felt sure had nothing to do with driving.

Any signage in the vehicle was in Swiss German, so that didn't help Blotto at all. But the fact that one of the controls had a trigger he thought was a bit of a giveaway. Also, adjacent to it was a deep slot, a giant version of the kind through which balls could be fed into a bagatelle board, ready to be shot out in hopes of scoring.

Even someone stupider than Blotto (presuming that, after a fairly long search, one could be found) would have recognised this to be a breech-loading mechanism.

The only question that arose in his mind was: what was a boddo meant to load the wodjermabit with?

Two stout boxes behind the passenger seat supplied the answer. They looked like containers for ammunition and that was exactly what they proved to be. The larger one was full of yellow orbs, cushioned in cotton wool. They were about the size of cricket balls and Blotto, who still had his bat with him, felt an overpowering urge to hit one of them with it. But they felt flabby and rubbery in his hand, and he knew he couldn't score a six with something so soft.

So, conquering the urge, instead he rolled a ball into the loading channel. It slid smoothly out of sight and a metallic click suggested that it had found its destination in the firing mechanism. All that remained was to see what would happen when the trigger was pulled.

Blotto, like anyone on a military mission, assessed his position. The end of the barrel protruding from the front of his vehicle was only a couple of yards from the garage door through which he'd entered. Though the ball he had loaded did not look as if it would have much destructive power, it might have been designed to wreak all kinds of havoc. Would firing the projectile in such a confined space be the responsible thing to do?

This moral qualm only slowed him down for a moment. Though far from being the sharpest arrow in the quiver, Blotto could sometimes be surprisingly logical in working things out. Despite having had little time to think about it, the conviction was growing in him that his 'accident' on the Croissant Run had been the result of sabotage.

And he had a strong suspicion as to who might have arranged that sabotage. What other reason could Ulrich Weissfeder have had for being in the Croissant Run clubroom just before Blotto's attempt on Lewdie's record?

Also, Ulrich Weissfeder, Blotto had worked out, was in cahoots with Count von Strapp, the owner of Chäs Luzvimmen. They'd both played him a diddler's hand. So, as a form of revenge, any damage done to the premises of the cheese manufacturer was more than justified.

Strengthened by this conclusion, Blotto put his hand on the firing mechanism and pulled the trigger. The percussive sound ruled out any lingering possibility that the vehicle was not a weapon of war.

Well, that's a wocky rum baba, he thought, as he looked at the results of his cannonade.

The soft ball of cheese had done what one would expect a soft ball of cheese to do when hurled with great velocity against a garage door. It had splatted against it and flattened out to form a perfect sticky circle about ten times the diameter of the ball before firing.

And, Blotto noted with a rueful grin of inevitability, the large circle of cheese attached to the garage door had holes in it.

Then he noticed something more sinister. Having attached itself to the metal surface, the substance did not remain the same size. The edges spread, somehow increasing in volume about tenfold from the original circle. The projectile's aim was not just to hit its target but to spread all over it. If that target happened to be a human being, they would be very quickly immobilised.

The work-out in the Chapel of the Secret Order, which Twinks and Gretchen were witnessing, was becoming more vigorous by the minute. The two defrocked . . . or, perhaps more accurately, un-habited . . . nuns had dropped the 'Make us stronger!' incantation and were now doing all their ever-accelerating movements to the unison chant of, 'We will defeat the Holy Temptation!'

'Do you know what the spoffing "Holy Temptation" is when it's got its spats on?' Twinks whispered urgently to Gretchen.

'Er . . . no,' came the response.

The hesitation was enough to tell Twinks the finishing school pupil was lying.

For the first time, she wondered how far she could trust Gretchen Kohlschuffler. Had she walked into another trap?

* * *

Having seen the capabilities of the large soft balls, Blotto addressed himself to the other box of ammunition. The contents here were different. Hard for a start, and much smaller, about the size of rabbit droppings. They had no packing around them and rattled like gravel. But opening up their container had made the atmosphere in the vehicle even cheesier.

To feed just one of the pellets into the loading breech looked stupid, so Blotto poured down a handful, rather as he used to cram rusty nails into the trumpet mouth of an old Tawcester Towers blunderbuss. He heard no satisfying click from the mechanism in front of him, so he added another handful. That got the click.

Once again, sighting along the barrel, Blotto squeezed the trigger.

The shot rang out and the pellets peppered the garage door. They took a bit of yellow paint off but caused no greater damage.

Blotto was confused. He couldn't think what military purpose such feeble projectiles could serve. He put a few of the smaller pellets into his trouser pocket. Maybe Twinks would be able to explain their purpose. Or Corky Froggett might have an idea. The chauffeur was, after 'the recent little dust-up in France', something of an expert on mechanised weaponry.

As he had this thought, Blotto heard a sound. The garage door he'd just shot at was opening.

Framed by it, Ulrich Weissfeder approached. Behind him were a dozen of Count von Strapp's black-clad guards. All carried pistols.

And their pistols were all pointing straight at Blotto's heart.

13

Double Jeopardy

It was a good fight. When was the Honourable Devereux Lyminster ever involved in a fight that wasn't a good one? And, though one man with a cricket bat against twelve armed with pistols were the kind of odds he liked, mathematical superiority was always going to tell. Only not in his favour.

But Blotto gave a good account of himself, and many of his opponents were soon nursing bruised heads, fingers, knees and elbows from the flashing blade of his cricket bat. Interestingly, none of his assailants showed any intention of using their pistols. Though deduction wasn't his forte, Blotto did deduce from this that they were under instructions to take him alive.

So . . . Count von Strapp had definitely tried to organise his coffination on the Croissant Run, but he now had other plans. What these might be, Blotto was too brave to think about.

Soon he was trussed up like a chicken, bundled into a horse-drawn sleigh and, guarded by the servants in black, taken up the mountain for incarceration in Schloss Luzvimmen.

Twinks was suspicious of Gretchen Kohlschuffler, but now it appeared that Gretchen Kohlschuffler was also suspicious of Twinks. 'I think you know full well,' the girl said in a fierce whisper, 'the meaning of the Holy Temptation.'

'I haven't a mouse-squeak of an idea,' Twinks protested. 'If I had, I wouldn't be popping the q to you about it, would I?'

'I think you are doing that only to find out how much we here in the Convent of the Sacred Icicle know about the Holy Temptation.'

'Why, in the name of Wilberforce, would I want to do that?'

'Because you are a spy,' said Gretchen. 'You have been infiltrated into the Convent of the Sacred Icicle to spy on us.'

'And what, in the name of snitchrags, am I meant to be spying on?'

'This.' Gretchen Kohlschuffler gestured down to the centre of the Chapel of the Secret Order, where the two nuns still continued their exhausting regime. 'You have come to spy on us to see how far we are ahead.'

'How far you are ahead?' Twinks echoed. 'Gretchen, you are talking complete gubbins. Unadulterated meringue. With the best will in the world, I think you're a case for the bonkers-doctor.'

'I am not talking complete gubbins!' In her fury at the accusation, Gretchen forgot to whisper.

The reaction was immediate. Down in the Chapel of the Secret Order, two shocked faces looked up towards them.

As Twinks turned to flee, the door through which they'd entered the gallery opened.

Outlined in it, looking extremely vindictive, stood Sister Benedicta and Sister Dagmar.

'I can do what I like with you,' said Count von Strapp from underneath his eyebrows. His English was accented but punctiliously correct. 'No one from your famous British diplomatic service will lift a finger to help you. No country has any loyalty to its spies.'

'Are you calling me a spoffing spy?' asked a furious Blotto. 'That's way beyond the running rail!'

'What else should I call someone who has the brazen gall to break into my cheese-processing works?'

'I did not break in, in the name of ginger,' Blotto protested. 'One of the doors was open.'

'Very well.' The Count smiled a patronising smile. 'You were not "breaking and entering". But you were still entering private property without permission. Here in Switzerland, that is an offence. And entering private property without permission for the purpose of spying is a much more serious offence.'

'Put me on trial for it then!' said Blotto defiantly. 'I can prove that I wasn't spying!' He wasn't sure that he could, but he felt sure Twinks would have some stratagemette to get him off the gaff.

'I am not bothered with trials,' said the Count. 'Except, of course, trials of my chemical inventions. Here in Luzvimmen, I am judge and jury. In fact, I am judge and jury in the whole of Europe, probably the whole of the world! When I decide what should be done with someone who crosses me, it will be done, swiftly and efficiently. As will your death, *Blotto*.' He put a particularly snide intonation on the name.

'I have a particularly effective device for eliminating my enemies. Behind the doors over there. It is called the Cheese Grater. And it destroys a human body in such a way that it leaves no trace at all. That will be your fate, Blotto, when I think the moment is right.

'And not a sound of protest will be heard. The waters of history will close over your head, as if you had never existed.'

'You don't appear,' Blotto came back coolly, 'to recognise who you're up against, if you think you can take the jam off my biscuit so easily. I don't care a tuppenny farthing for your threats. Because I'm a Lyminster, and the Lyminsters, over the centuries, have been like the skin on a boddo's cocoa. We always come out on top. Whoever's trying to put lumps in our custard, we always end up at the top of the cocoa mug.' (Blotto didn't know what a mixed metaphor was and, if he had known, that wouldn't have stopped him using them.)

'You should realise by now, Count, that – whatever kind of diddler's hand you try to play – you're never going to hobble the heels of a Lyminster. We have come out on top in the Norman Conquest, the Wars of the Roses, the English Civil War and the Tawcestershire Best Crenellations Competition. That fumacious lump of toad-spawn Weissfeder tried to coffinate me on the Croissant Run. And he was about as successful as a blancmange in a boxing match. Try your worst, Count! I'm not frightened of you and your Cheese Grater! You are up against a Lyminster! All Lyminsters are Grade A foundation stones! And all Lyminsters are spoffing indestructible!'

Blotto was rather pleased with this peroration but Count

von Strapp looked singularly unimpressed. '"Indestruct-ible"?' he echoed with a harsh laugh. 'You may have been indestructible to every hazard that has so far been invented. But no one is proof against the effect of my weapons of destruction!'

The Count looked out with satisfaction through the large window of his operation centre. He gestured to the town of Luzvimmen. 'All this,' he said, 'I could destroy in seconds.'

'Oh yes? And how would you achieve that if some boddo wanted to stop you? Tell.'

Blotto was surprised by the effect that word had. 'I knew it!' the Count roared. 'I knew you were spying for him! For the one whose name is not to be spoken.'

'Sorry, I'm not reading your semaphore,' said a bewildered Blotto.

'All my enemies I could destroy in seconds!' Foam spattered through the eyebrows. 'And when the time is right, that is what I will do. But you will have the honour of being the first to suffer!'

'Not in a month of Tuesdays!' cried Blotto. 'Slugbuckets like you think you can take over the spoffing world. You—'

'I've had enough of this!' snapped Count von Strapp, now speaking in Swiss German. 'Guards, take him to the Sealed Unit!'

Though he resisted manfully, sheer force of numbers meant the black-clad guards soon had him immobilised.

'And take away his cricket bat!' said the Count.

Broken biscuits, thought Blotto mournfully. Talk about kicking a man when he's down. Foreigners just didn't get it. They should all be put through English public school. Then they'd have some concept of the right colours to flick up the flagpole.

* * *

138

Twinks was not going to take on Sister Benedicta and Sister Dagmar. It wasn't that she didn't think she could evade their clutches. It was more that she was in the same space as Aurelia ffrench-Windeau, the object of her quest to Switzerland. Who could say when she would next have an opportunity to speak to the girl?

So, she rushed down the stairs from the gallery on to the floor of the Chapel of the Secret Order. Still in shock, the two nuns had not resumed their physical jerks. Sister Liselotte was taken aback to be dragged off her wheeled boards by a schoolgirl with squeezable spots whom she hadn't seen before.

'Listen, Aurelia,' Twinks hissed before she could be interrupted, 'I have to know what's going on.'

'I am at my devotions,' the girl replied doggedly. Her look of infuriating serenity had reasserted itself.

'Snubbins to your devotions!' said Twinks. 'I'm Twinks, as you know full well. Your sister Berry's chumbo. And Berry's got her worry-boots in a proper cat's cradle about you.'

'I can't worry what Berry thinks.'

'You don't have to, by Denzil!' Twinks improvised madly. 'That was the gin-gen I wanted to uncage to you. I've written to Berry to say that you're as safe as a duck in orange. That you're going to twiddle the old reef-knot with Christ and that your behaviour in future will be as pure as driven sheep. Don't don your worry-boots, Aurelia. Your sister and mother both know that you're now a "GLG".'

It had the desired effect. The insult instantly drained the girl's face of serenity and replaced it with the sheer vindictiveness of the Devil of the Dorms.

'Look, if you think I—'

But Aurelia's protestations were cut short as Twinks was

139

manhandled – or, more accurately, womanhandled – away by Sister Anneliese-Marie, Sister Benedicta and Sister Dagmar.

The Sealed Unit was exactly that. Down at the dungeon level of Schloss Luzvimmen, where the cows were milked continuously winter and summer, Blotto had been bundled into it by the Count's acolytes in black. He found himself immured in a space about the size of the Tawcester Towers boot room. Walls, ceiling and floor were all uniformly polished rock, the surface so smooth that he could not even see the outline of the door through which he had been pushed. There was light, but he couldn't detect its source, and a flow of fresh air. Though where that was coming from, he couldn't see either.

Though Blotto's spirits had the permanent buoyancy of a beach ball, he did feel a cloud of gloom crossing his seaside horizon at that moment. He didn't understand what was going on (a common affliction which rarely caused him anxiety), and he didn't know what was going to happen next (a permanent situation which he usually approached with gleeful insouciance but which on this occasion was giving him a touch of the wibbles).

He knew he wouldn't be feeling so low if the slug-buckets hadn't taken his cricket bat.

Basically, he needed Twinks there to point his prow in the right direction.

The Mother Superior was no fool. She saw through Twinks's make-up and did not for a moment believe her to be Sylviane Heffelfinger. In fact, she very quickly identified the intruder as Lady Honoria Lyminster.

'You are a determined young woman,' she said, once Twinks had been removed to a punishment cell which had a great deal of locking ironmongery on its doors. 'But I have been aware of your movements since you first arrived in Luzvimmen. When I saw you had disguised yourself as one of the convent's pupils, I arranged for Gretchen Kohlschuffler to keep an eye on you. She did her job well. She recognised that you were a spy from the Holy Temptation.'

'I've never heard a mouse-squeak about the Holy Temptation! What is it when it's got its spats on?'

'There's no point in pretending with me, Lady Honoria. I know exactly why you're here and I'm going to see to it that you don't betray any information about our plans to the Holy Temptation.'

'Since I don't know what the fumacious Holy Temptation is, I'm hardly going to—'

'Be quiet!' bellowed Sister Anneliese-Marie. 'You are now going to be immured in here until you can do no further harm to our endeavour. Because this is a punishment cell, you will only be fed bread and water. That will be delivered through the slot in the door here. Sister Benedicta, Sister Dagmar – lock her in!'

The doors were slammed shut after the retreating Mother Superior. The two nuns got to work on clicking and slamming and slotting in the ironmongery of locks.

Twinks waited until they had disappeared down the corridor before pulling her sequined reticule out of her skirt and taking out the relevant picklocks.

* * *

141

In the Sealed Unit, Blotto was bored. He was always bored when he hadn't got any physical outlet for his phenomenal energy. He did five hundred press-ups to consume some of it, but then he got bored with doing press-ups.

When he had no access to the great outdoors, he wasn't a man of many resources. Without access to cricket, hunting, and knocking vicars off bicycles in the Lagonda, he was at a very loose end. If the Sealed Unit had boasted a library, that wouldn't have been much use to him either. He'd had to read a book while he was at Eton, but hadn't made a habit of it. One was plenty.

He sat on the smooth stone floor and picked his own brains. That didn't take long. He tried to think of something else to do.

He went through the trouser pockets of his tweed suit. A rather grubby handkerchief and a rather furry toffee. He took one look and decided to hold it back as emergency supplies for when he was really hungry.

He tried his jacket pockets and found the Swiss German leaflet with the picture of people skiing on it, and the pellets he'd taken from the tank in the yellow buildings. A rather nauseating aroma emanated from them. Inevitably, cheese. He wondered, if the hunger pangs became irresistible, whether he'd be reduced to eating one of them.

The sound of soft feet running along the corridor towards her stopped Twinks in her lock-picking exercise. She shuffled the equipment back under her skirt.

The visitor was a finishing school pupil whom Twinks had not seen before. She carried a small leatherbound book which looked like a missal or hymnal. This the girl put

142

through the slot into the cell with the breathless words in Swiss German, 'This is from Sister Liselotte. It is to assist your devotions.'

With that, the girl turned round and scurried off.

Twinks handled the book gently. It had a brass lock on it, like a secret diary. Engraved on the front in gold letters were the words, 'LOST ARE THE ESTEEMS OF LORD CHRIST'. Some biblical text, but not, surprisingly, one that she recognised. (Which was unusual because, of course, Twinks did know everything.)

But Twinks was more interested in the book's contents. Not its printed pages; she was looking for something more.

And she found it without having to resort to the picklocks in her sequined reticule. She saw a protruding edge of paper, which had been tucked away in the back cover. She pulled out a much-flattened piece of handwritten paper.

With a mixture of excitement and trepidation, Twinks unfolded it.

Blotto was not quite so bored now. He had something to engage what passed for his mind. He remembered some beak at Eton once using the expression 'a moral dilemma'. And Blotto reckoned that's exactly what he'd got.

The kind of thing that Greek philosophers would argue about endlessly. Plateau, Soccertogs, Arisbottle and that lot.

In the event of hunger, ran Blotto's Socratic Dialogue with himself, which would I eat first – the furry toffee or one of the cheesy pellets?

That represented a moral dilemma if ever there was one.

14

United in Doom

Twinks's perusal of what she was sure was a vital message from Aurelia ffrench-Windeau was prevented by the sound of more footsteps coming her way along the corridor outside her cell. It was a matter of moments to secrete book and folded paper inside her sequined reticule and to have that whisked out of sight under her schoolgirl skirt.

She looked up to see the reappearance of the Mother Superior, flanked by Sisters Benedicta and Dagmar. Sister Anneliese-Marie opened the unlocked cell door with a wry grin. 'I might have expected you would have found a way to get out of here.'

'Give that pony a rosette,' said Twinks, with all the charm she could muster.

'It just confirms my view,' said the Mother Superior, mirroring Twinks's smile with an ironic one of her own, 'that it is dangerous to have you under the roof of the Convent of the Sacred Icicle. The Holy Temptation is not going to get all of our secrets so easily.'

'At the risk of putting the same cylinder on again,' said

Twinks patiently, 'I haven't a bar of Sunlight Soap's idea what the Holy Temptation is.'

'Well, fortunately,' came the response, 'we won't have to listen to your pathetic protestations much longer. Though this cell is adequate for the incarceration of a misbehaving novice, you clearly demand more robust security arrangements. So, I am going see you're locked up somewhere that is completely impossible to escape from.'

'And am I allowed to have a twingle of an idea where that might be?'

'No,' said the Mother Superior.

Blotto was actually getting quite hungry now. The necessary fuel for his boundless energy was three substantial (very substantial) meals a day. Being deprived of any of these was one of the few events which could deflect his emotional barometer from its default setting of 'Sunny'.

So, his Socratic Dialogue about choosing between the furry toffee and the cheesy pellet was moving from the theoretical to the practical. His rumbling stomach required a resolution of the dilemma.

Closer inspection of the toffee revealed that it really was *quite* furry. It was hard to guess what varied species of dust it had rubbed against during its long incarceration in the pocket of Blotto's tweed jacket. Indeed, it was entirely possible that the toffee predated Blotto's inheritance of the suit. It could be a toffee that the late Duke of Lyminster had secreted there, so as not to affect the aim of his duck gun when out wildfowling many decades before.

The toffee was not, in fact, an alluring sight.

Blotto reached into his pocket to extract one of the

pellets. Shrinking from the strong smell, he raised it to his lips.

But before he could put it in his mouth, he was distracted by the sound of the Sealed Unit's door opening.

Twinks found it undignified that she'd been gagged in the horse-drawn sleigh during her transfer from the Convent of the Sacred Icicle. But, at the same time, she was slightly flattered. Sister Anneliese-Marie had insisted on the gagging, because she was afraid Sisters Benedicta and Dagmar might be seduced by Twinks's silver tongue into allowing her to escape.

The gag was not taken off when the prisoner was handed over, at the agreed meeting point, to another set of guards in another horse-drawn sleigh.

Twinks still had it on when she was pushed into a featureless cell in the lower reaches of Schloss Luzvimmen.

And when she saw her brother about to pop something like a rabbit dropping into his mouth.

Blotto's mood was instantly transformed. Even the pangs of hunger felt less pressing now Twinks was with him. Yes, all right, they were in a fumacious gluepot, incarcerated in the bowels of a Swiss Schloss by a set of eyebrows bidding to take over the world, but with his sister on the prems, everything would soon be creamy éclair. Twinks could turn any cloud round and show the silver.

She, however, seemed more thoughtful. Though obviously ecstatic at being reunited with her brother, she wasn't immediately bursting out with Grandissimos!,

Splendissimos!, Larkssissimos! and Jollissimos! Which was unusual for Twinks.

'I think,' said Blotto, 'the minute we get out of this swamphole, we leap in the Lag and pongle, quick as a lizard's lick, straight back to the Land of the Golden Lions.' He stopped for a moment. 'Though, does that mean we'll be back at the Towers for Christmas? That might put the Mater in crimps, don't you think? It'll really put the crud in the crumpet for her if—'

'Blotto, will you stuff a pillow in it!'

He was totally shocked. Never, in some decades of siblinghood, had his sister actually shouted at him. She had certainly been provoked sufficiently to do so, but some caring instinct had always curbed her tongue when her brother made a dungheap of things. Growing up at Tawcester Towers in the face of their mother's indifference had made the two very protective of each other.

The fact that Twinks had let rip at Blotto at that moment was a measure of how serious she thought the situation in which they had found themselves.

She was instantly all apology. 'Blotters, for the love of snitchrags, I didn't mean to toggle your turn-ups. Sorry, trip of the tongue-trap. I'm a total numbnoddy. Poked my cue in the wrong pocket. Can you ever find it in your heartlet to forgive me?'

'Yes, of course, Twinks me old marmalade slicer,' he said. 'No skin off my rice pudding.' But the pain still lingered.

'Blotto me old bootscraper, if you could just give your sis a couple of momentettes of silence, I've got something here I've got to pop the peepers over, which may straighten out the corkscrew on what's going on in this horracious place?'

She produced the folded paper from the back of the missal and waved it at her brother. 'This, I hope, can declog

147

the incog. With a bit of luck, the whole sit will soon be as clear as consommé. So, if you wouldn't mind jamming a gag in it for a couple of mins . . .'

'I'll be as tight as a limpet with lockjaw,' said Blotto, still not fully mollified.

Twinks scanned the paper. As she had hoped, it came from Aurelia and was written in her rather childlike writing. This is what Twinks read:

'First, I am not and never have been a GLG! I'm jolly cross that you should even mention the idea. And even crosser that you should dare to describe me in that way to my sister. After such a bouncer, it's going to take a long time before I can get back to the way Berry and I normally behave together. Which is to say, permanently insulting each other.

'I suppose, Twinks, you want some explanation of what's going on with me. All this talk of "devotions" and me being "a Bride of Christ" and all that gubbins must feel pretty strange to you. It feels pretty strange to me, too, but take my word for it, it's the only way I'm going to get what I want out of life.

'Haven't you ever had to do something difficult to get what you really want? That's the situation I'm in now. I suppose what's odd is that I have never before known so clearly what I do want in life. Oh, certainly there were things I wanted – alcohol, cigarettes, boys, generally annoying people. But it's only since I've been at the Convent of the Sacred Icicle that I've known the one really big thing I want.

'I can't tell you what it is now. For the time being, it has to be kept under wraps. And, sadly, for me those "wraps" mean going along with all this religious nonsense about the Secret Order. Soon I'll be able to stop all that, but I can't yet, if I'm going to achieve my ambition.

'Tomorrow morning is the important date. Get tomorrow morning over and, if we can defeat the Holy Temptation, then I can reorganise my life, even think about getting back to the Land of the Golden Lions and recommencing hostilities with Berry.

'Once we've got tomorrow morning over, I can explain everything to you, Twinks.

'Love, Aurelia (the Devil of the Dorms – really, I promise).'

Twinks put the paper down on her lap and murmured thoughtfully to herself, 'Holy Temptation.' She looked at her brother and repeated the words, 'Holy Temptation. Does that mean anything to you, Blotto?'

'Well, I'd stake my last frayed bow-tie on the fact that it's something Swiss.'

'Would you, by Denzil?' asked Twinks, unused to receiving insight from that particular source. 'What makes you say that?'

'Well, every other fumacious thing they make is holey. I mean, you have only to look at the cheese.'

Twinks curbed her disappointment. It had been too much to hope that Blotto had received a sudden injection of perspicacity.

Blotto didn't say anything else. His sister had, after all, told him to stuff a pillow in it. Growing up with the Dowager Duchess had taught him that there were times when a boddo should not speak until spoken to. He was a little cast down to find himself in that situation with Twinks, though.

His sister put down the handwritten note and turned her attention to the missal in which it had arrived. She examined the exterior – neat leather binding, brass hasp locking it and the inscription in gold lettering. 'LOST ARE THE ESTEEMS OF LORD CHRIST'.

Suddenly realisation struck her. She tapped her beautiful forehead, frustrated by her slowness.

'English!' she announced.

'Yes, of course I am,' said Blotto. 'Is the King German? And I just feel sorry for all those poor droplets who got the wrong end of the sink plunger by not being English.'

While appreciating the generosity of her brother's sentiment, Twinks needed to move on. 'No, I wasn't talking about you, Blotters me old penny-farthing. I was talking about this book.'

'Tickey-tockey.' He could never pretend to have much interest in books.

Twinks had extracted the picklocks from her sequined reticule and was making quick work of the tiny lock. She opened the book and flicked through the pages. 'Ah. English, too,' she said knowingly.

Blotto didn't say anything. He thought he had made a full expression of his views on Englishness. There was nothing to add.

After a quick perusal, Twinks said, 'It's a bit of rum baba. Settle your seeing apparatus on this, Blotters me old straw boater.'

Blotto looked inside the missal Twinks had thrust at him. 'It's all spoffing advice about how to ski,' he said in disappointment after a few minutes. 'For the kind of poor thimbles who don't know that stuff instinctively.' He did not of course count himself in that category. Although he had yet even to put on a pair of skis, he reckoned he'd be able to have a yeoman's punt at it. How difficult could it be? Just a matter of a boddo keeping balance. Stay steady and it'd all be creamy éclair.

'But why,' asked Twinks, 'would a ladleful of nuns want to learn about skiing?'

But even as she asked the question, answers to it were beginning to blossom in her brain.

Despite the comforts of Heidi Finnischann's hayloft, Corky Froggett could not be said to be entirely happy in Luzvimmen. Separation from the young master and the young mistress never agreed with him. He kept worrying that they might be threatened by some mortal danger, and he would miss the opportunity to do what his entire life had been preparing him for – laying down that life in their defence.

He was also worried about the Lagonda. Despite his assiduous cleaning morning and evening, Corky feared that the frosts of Luzvimmen were not doing any good to the precious blue bodywork. He was even more concerned about the cold bringing potential harm to the car than he was about it bringing potential harm to his moustache (and that was saying something).

Another source of anxiety was the current absence of the young master and the young mistress. Corky Froggett knew his place and did not expect to be kept informed of his employers' every move, but it did strike him that he hadn't seen either of them for a while. He decided to check at the reception desk of the Hotel Luzvimmen.

When travelling abroad, the chauffeur behaved in the manner of the majority of his fellow countrymen and -women. Specimens like Twinks, who could actually speak any foreign languages, were few and far between. Fewer and even further between were those to whom the idea of speaking a foreign language ever occurred. So, Corky followed the unalterable rule: Speak English and, in the event that anyone appears not to understand you, speak English louder.

With the receptionist at the Hotel Luzvimmen, he did not have to go to the second stage. The girl knew exactly what he was asking and replied in only slightly accented English.

'You say ... Lord Devereux and Lady Honoria Lyminster?' The girl opened a large ledger on her desk.

'That is correct, yes.'

'And you wish to know their current whereabouts?'

'That is correct, yes.' No point in using a different formula of words. They'd worked first time.

The girl ran her finger down the handwritten listings till she found what she was looking for. Then announced, 'Lord Devereux and Lady Honoria Lyminster checked out of the hotel this morning.'

Corky Froggett smelt a rat. His employers would never leave Luzvimmen without telling him of their intentions. Nor would they go without asking him to bring the Lag round to the front of the hotel.

Another fact that made him uneasy was that, during 'the recent little dust-up in France', the expression 'check out' had taken on a meaning far different from just vacating a hotel room.

15

The Phantom Skiers

Heidi Finnischann's working shifts at Schloss Luzvimmen varied from day to day. So many cows were kept in the dungeons there that they had to be milked in relays. Sometimes she had to report for duty at six, sometimes later in the evening.

That day her call was for 10 p.m. At first she was uncertain about the idea of infiltrating Corky into her place of work, but he soon persuaded her to let him come with her. She would let him in by the staff entrance to the cows' cellars and show him where the spare black uniforms were kept. After that, he'd be on his own.

Having grown up there, Heidi knew the area well. From her parents' home in the village, they had to travel towards the Schloss up a steep incline, peppered with single fir trees. The snow solidified on their branches and turned them into white cones in the white landscape.

Heidi Finnischann didn't travel by sledge or skis, relying instead on her stout walking boots. The winters in Luzvimmen were so cold that the surface of the snow was frozen solid. Heidi and Corky could travel on top of it

153

without sinking. Once the thaw began, progress would become a lot more difficult.

The night was crisp and still, the moon imparting a blueish tinge to everything. There was something ghostly about the light. Whether that was the reason or not, Heidi found herself telling Corky about the legend of Saint Liselotte and the Phantom Skiers. It was a story that she had grown up with and, having drunk a fair bit of peasant credulity with her mother's milk, it was one she believed in implicitly. She also believed the old folk myth about Wilhelm Tell returning one day to save Switzerland from unknown disasters.

'There are two Avengers,' Heidi told Corky, 'locked in the glacier at the Convent of the Sacred Icicle. If anyone threatens the safety of Luzvimmen, the Avengers will be freed from their bonds and wreak awful revenge on the perpetrators of the atrocity.'

'Oh yes?' said the chauffeur. The girl appeared not to have noticed the profound cynicism of his tone. Corky Froggett was a man who dealt with the real world and, except for one occasion when he had started to believe that ducks had godlike powers, he kept his feet firmly on the ground.

'The Avengers,' Heidi went on, 'are also known as the Phantom Skiers. And, when I walk by night to my work at Schloss Luzvimmen, I am always afraid of meeting them.'

'Why's that?' asked Corky. 'I thought you said their mission was to protect the people of the village.'

'Yes, it is. But there is a rumour that, if they encounter anyone walking in the area after dark, they immediately decide that that person is up to no good and unleash their cruelty on them.'

'I see,' said Corky, his voice once again larded with

cynicism. He hadn't time for old wives' tales. 'Well, listen, Heidi, if they give us any trouble tonight, don't you worry about a thing. I'll see the stenchers off.'

'I don't think your power will be as strong as theirs.'

'My power, darling,' he said with complete confidence, 'is stronger than anyone's, alive or dead.' He didn't think it was the moment to admit that, actually, Blotto's was even stronger.

'Oh, Corky,' said Heidi, 'I am so lucky to have you here to protect me.' But she still didn't think he could defeat the Phantom Skiers.

'You certainly are, doll,' he said, with a smile of satisfaction. He liked the atavistic thrill of being the he-man guarding his womenfolk at the mouth of their cave.

He hoped Heidi had finished talking about local superstitions, but no, she went on. 'The Two Avengers are particularly protectors of Saint Liselotte. If anyone desecrates her memory, they will feel the Two Avengers' wrath.'

'Bad luck,' said Corky, with the minimum of interest.

'Saint Liselotte was martyred, you see.'

'Was she?'

'Yes, Corky. She was killed by the wicked Count, using a weapon that left no trace.'

'Oh,' said the chauffeur, in a tone of disappointment. 'Leaving no trace takes away the fun of killing people. During the recent little dust-up in France, there was nothing I enjoyed more than being behind my Accrington-Murphy machine gun, watching the enemy being blasted to blazes.' He noticed that Heidi did not appear to be sharing his enthusiasm. 'So, what was this weapon that left no trace?'

'It was an icicle,' she replied. 'It is because of the weapon used to kill the holy martyr Saint Liselotte that the convent in Luzvimmen is called the Convent of the Sacred Icicle.'

'Ah,' said Corky. He remembered hearing from Blotto that Twinks was investigating something in the local convent. Might be worth continuing his search for her there ... ?

'Is that the only convent round here?' he asked.

'No, there is another,' Heidi replied. 'In a nearby village. There is a ferocious rivalry between that one and the Convent of the Sacred Icicle.'

'Rivalry about what?'

'Everything. Which of them is more holy. Which of them has more sacred relics. In which of them do the nuns do more painful forms of penance. Which of them's choir sings better. Which of them has the more successful finishing school. Which of them serves up blander food for its English pupils. You name it, they argue about it.'

'And what is this other convent called?' asked Corky.

Heidi replied, 'The Convent of the Holy Temptation.'

Inside the Sealed Unit, Blotto was once again feeling hungry. He was relieved that Twinks was there, though. She was bound to have some ideas about sourcing food. At the very least, she could apply her brainpower to the tricky moral dilemma as to whether he should eat the furry toffee or one of the pellets first.

She was very interested when he produced one of the latter from his jacket pocket. He had to relate, in great detail, where and how he had found them. She also asked about the larger, softer ball which he had fired from the yellow tank's barrel, and the effect the smaller projectiles had had on the inside of the garage door.

156

She took a pellet from him and lifted it to her beautifully shaped nose.

'Smells of fumacious cheese,' Blotto offered.

'Yes, it spoffing well does,' his sister agreed. She felt the small spheroid between finger and thumb. 'But harder than any cheese I've ever encountered. Harder than Parmesan, harder than Pecorino Romano. Hm ... Now, I wonder what this flipmadoodle is when it's got its spats on? Well, I can soon find out.'

She turned to her sequined reticule and produced from it a complete science kit, comprising a microscope, scalpels, tweezers, and a series of stoppered bottles containing chemicals. Blotto resigned himself to the fact that it would be some time before his immediate problem was addressed. When his sister got involved in an experiment, mere details like hunger got ignored.

His stomach rumbled in protest, but Twinks didn't hear it.

Corky and Heidi were getting quite close to Schloss Luzvimmen when they saw them. Speeding down from higher up the mountainside, two figures in black robes. Two figures in black robes on skis. Almost side by side, they skirted the trees, leaning at angles the human body was not designed for. And at speeds the human body wasn't designed for either.

The chauffeur and milkmaid stood frozen in every literal and metaphorical sense of the word. Then, as the two figures accelerated closer, Heidi, with a cry of 'It's the Two Avengers!', ran, slithered and skidded off back towards her home.

Corky Froggett stood his ground, ready to face any

challenge, be it from human or ghost. His moustache bristled in anticipation of violence.

But none ensued. The black-robed figures went shooting past, possibly not even having noticed he was there. They disappeared, still weaving in and out of the fir trees, on their glissade down the mountain.

Corky Froggett shrugged. He had no idea what was going on and didn't care. The only thing he did know was that the two skiers had been human beings. Nothing to do with phantoms.

He trudged on towards Schloss Luzvimmen. Heidi Finnischann had pointed out the staff entrance to him. Once inside, he knew where to find that black uniform which was to be his disguise.

Then he would rescue the young master and the young mistress. He felt sure that they were prisoners of Count von Strapp.

Twinks's experiments seemed to be taking a long time, but Blotto knew better than to interrupt her concentration. Though it cost some effort, he was as silent as a gagged Trappist. He knew he wouldn't get any attention from her until she had finished. His empty stomach rumbled disconsolately. Still, his sister did not hear it.

He vaguely watched what she was doing but didn't ask for explanations. Experience had taught him that he wouldn't understand a word.

At one point, Twinks poured a little fluid from one of the bottles into a shallow dish and held a sliver of cheese pellet over it. 'I may be rouletting the risk here a tidge, Blotters,' she said, 'but I have to find out the truth. If what I'm about to do blows us on a quick route to the Pearlies,

158

then I can only say being your sister has all been creamy éclair – and thanks for the whole clangdumble.'

'Similar likewise,' said Blotto, not at all sure what was going on.

Taking a deep breath, Twinks dropped the scrap of pellet into the fluid. There was an immediate fierce sizzling sound as the fragment dried into the shape of a small black comma.

'Jollissimo!' she murmured. 'Just as I had calculated.'

Blotto suddenly became aware of the smell rising off the small dish. 'If my nose isn't sniggling me,' he said, 'that liquid you've got there is the pick of the punnet of fine old brandies.'

His sister did not deny it.

'Then could I quaff a slurpette of the gubbins?' asked Blotto. 'To stave off the gut-gripes?'

'No,' Twinks responded, with a firmness that was pure Dowager Duchess. 'None of this paraphernatus is to be used for anything other than legitimate scientific experiment.'

'Oh, snickets,' said Blotto disconsolately as she replaced the bottles in her sequined reticule.

From then on, he just watched in silence, as his sister continued slicing at the pellets, setting tiny slivers between glass to be inspected by the microscope, and generally giving a very good impersonation of a research chemist.

Finally, after what seemed to Blotto several millennia, or would have done if he'd known what the word meant, Twinks gave a very good impersonation of a research chemist who had completed her current experiment.

She sat back with satisfaction. 'I see exactly what backdoor-sidling the four-faced filcher is up to.'

'The four-faced filcher in question being the Count?' asked her brother.

'Bong on the nose, Blotters. What a total lump of toadspawn!'

'So, are the fumacious pellets made of cheese?'

'Two bongs on your nose.'

'Swiss cheese?'

'Third bong.'

'With wocky holes in it?'

'That, Blotto me old chisel-sharpener, is where the sit becomes interesting.'

But not as interesting to her brother as the scrapings of cheese pellet on the bench she'd been working on. His hunger going into overdrive, he reached out towards the scraps.

Blotto felt sudden pain from a slap across his knuckles. 'Not on your nuthatch!' snapped Twinks. 'Whatever you do, don't put any of that gubbins in your mouth!'

Inside the Sealed Unit, Twinks took another look at the cover of the skiing manual. In particular, at the engraved inscription. 'LOST ARE THE ESTEEMS OF LORD CHRIST'.

'Have you got a mouse-squeak of an idea what that might mean, Blotters?' she asked, more to make conversation than in the hope of getting an answer that might solve the conundrum.

'Well, it might mean,' her brother began cautiously, 'that some boddo called "The Lord Christ" . . .'

'Yes?' Twinks prompted.

'. . . has lost some Esteems . . .'

'Yes, it could mean that,' Twinks agreed without marked

enthusiasm. She once again focused her azure eyes, with their direct connection to her giant brain, on to the inscription.

Suddenly the scales fell from her eyes.

'What a numbnoddy I've been!' she said. 'What a pot-brained pineapple! I should have realised the moment I clapped my peepers on it!'

'What?' asked Blotto rather forlornly. He was used to being left behind in the wake of his sister's accelerating brain.

'It's not a spoffing quotation from the Bible,' she said. 'I thought there was something leadpenny about it! And I should have known, by Denzil, because if I didn't recognise it from the Bible, then it never hung up its jim-jams in there.'

'Good ticket,' said an uncomprehending Blotto.

'It's an anagram!' Twinks announced. 'Splendissimo!' A pause, then, 'You know what an anagram is, don't you, Blotto?'

'Yes,' he replied confidently. 'It's one of those musical wodjermabits that you play cylinders on.'

Though Heidi Finnischann was no longer with him, her instructions had been very exact, so Corky Froggett had no difficulty in finding the staff entrance to the dungeon level of Schloss Luzvimmen. Her diligent approach to her duties meant that – except when frightened off by Phantom Avengers – she always arrived early for her shifts. So, there was no one around when Corky sidled in.

He found the changing room where the black garments were kept. He selected a large size. He had no intention of taking off his chauffeur's uniform, so he needed one that would fit over it. Having dressed himself, he pulled a black cap down over his hair and moved out of the changing room.

He soon found himself surrounded by other black-clad figures. The change of shift meant that some were leaving and some arriving. None of them looked twice at the disguised chauffeur, as he set out to explore Schloss Luzvimmen.

Blotto was still puzzling over how a small leather-bound book could play music cylinders, as Twinks solved the anagram.

'Jollissimo!' she cried. 'That's turned the last tumbler!'

'Good ticket,' said Blotto. He had always found that an uncontroversial response when he hadn't a clue what someone was talking about.

'And,' his sister went on, 'it's unfogged the windscreen considerably.'

'Good ticket.' Well, it had worked once.

'What "LOST ARE THE ESTEEMS OF LORD CHRIST" is an anagram of is . . .'

Twinks paused for dramatic effect. Blotto, to be on the safe side, threw in another speculative 'Good ticket.'

His sister made her revelation: 'THE SECRET ORDER OF THE SLALOMISTS!'

16

Corky in the Schloss

One thing Corky Froggett had learnt during the recent little dust-up in France, which had also been of great use in his chauffeuring work, was the ability to look busy. On many occasions in the trenches, he had been suspected by senior officers of slacking but, however close their scrutiny, they always left convinced that he was doing something useful.

It was a valuable skill to have and a skill which helped considerably in his exploration of Schloss Luzvimmen's lower reaches. Everyone else there was busy with their allotted tasks, the black-clad herdsmen leading the cows from pens to milking sheds and back again, the black-clad milkmaids busy draining their udders of the essential ingredient for Chäs Luzvimmen. None of them showed any interest in the disguised chauffeur wandering in their midst.

As he continued his reconnaissance, Corky Froggett, though not prone to introspection, did question why he was so convinced that Schloss Luzvimmen contained the solution to his problem. To his ordered mind, it was quite logical. The young master and the young mistress were definitely missing. The report from the girl at the Hotel Luzvimmen reception that they'd 'checked out' was clearly a lie. And, amongst the many things Corky had learnt from Heidi Finnischann in her hayloft was the fact that everything in the village was ultimately controlled by Count von Strapp. It naturally followed that the missing siblings must be somewhere in his Schloss.

All he had to do was find them.

Strapped up in the sanatorium under Doktor Krankenschwindler's strict orders, Buffy 'Crocker' Wilmslow was also wondering what had happened to Blotto. Wouldn't have hurt the old muffin-toaster to pongle over and visit him, would it? Blotto had always been a Grade A foundation stone about gubbins like that.

Still, Crocker reflected mournfully, people can change. Life gets in the way, takes them off in other directions. Probably no chance Blotto would organise the appropriate revenge on Victor Muke-Wallingborough now, either.

'It's the original locked room mystery,' said Twinks disconsolately.

She had just finished a detailed examination of the Sealed Unit in which they were incarcerated. And, in spite of the armoury of house-breaking tools she had in her sequined reticule, she had not found the smallest crack or crevice into which a jemmy could be inserted. Annoyingly, she couldn't even find the outline of the door through which she had been thrust into the place. Whoever built the Sealed Unit – or carved it out of the craggy mountain stone – had done a frustratingly good job.

In her vain search for suitable tools in her sequined reticule, she came across the book on Wilhelm Tell she'd taken from the Hotel Luzvimmen library. Frustrated in her attempts to do anything more useful, she settled down to read it.

But her brother didn't think it was the moment for reading. As ever, he wanted action.

'Oh, rodents!' he said petulantly. 'Come on, sis, this is where you come up with a buzzbanger of an idea to get us out of this ghastible gluepot.'

'Well, I haven't got one,' said Twinks sourly. 'Not a bat-squeak of a thoughtette.' And she returned to finding out more about the Swiss folk hero Wilhelm Tell.

Blotto felt really let down. 'Broken biscuits!' he said. Which was a measure of just how let down he felt.

He even stamped his foot. Which was very childish.

But the thump of a heavy brogue on the floor did have an unexpected effect. A small square of stone rode up proud of the surface. 'Bring your jemmy here,' cried Blotto.

Casting her book aside, Twinks inserted the tool's metal edge under the loose slab and lifted it up. Revealed was a grille like the top of a drain. With that sight came, inevitably, a very strong smell of cheese.

Instantly, Twinks was looking up at the prison ceiling. 'What goes out of the spoffing bathtub must also go into it,' she said pensively.

She saw something. 'Give me a jockey-up on your shoulders, Blotters,' she said.

She was hoisted up as if she were as light as a dandelion seedhead and perched on her brother's shoulders. Her sharp eyes caught what they had missed on her first search. Again, a tiny square outline in the stone. Here the fit was so snug that she had difficulty in inserting the jemmy. But when she finally did, the cover dropped down as a small hinged flap.

What it exposed was a nozzle. Accompanied again by an overwhelming aroma of Chäs Luzvimmen.

'Toad-in-the-hole!' said Blotto triumphantly. 'We'll soon chip our way out of this and be rolling on camomile lawns.'

Twinks didn't say anything as she climbed down from her perch. She didn't want to dash her brother's hopes too quickly.

But, to her, their prospects looked very black. The openings for the nozzle and the drain were far too small to be of any use as escape routes. And nothing she had in her sequined reticule would be powerful enough to widen the apertures sufficiently to let out a full-sized human being. Dynamite could possibly do the job, but she hadn't got any. Also, its use might not do much for the health of the two people actually in the Sealed Unit.

She thought of something else that wouldn't do them much good either. She'd seen the system of tubes which sent molten cheese down from Schloss Luzvimmen to the yellow buildings at the foot of the mountain. Suppose part of that flow was diverted to come through the nozzle in the ceiling and fill up the Sealed Unit . . . ?

What a way to be coffinated! If, after all the dangers she'd been through in her life, the end came like that, she'd be really cheesed off.

Corky Froggett continued to apply his powers of logic to the situation. He planned everything like a military operation, still rueful that he wasn't participating in a real military operation, trigger-happy behind his Accrington-Murphy machine gun.

And suddenly, a recollection came to the aid of his logic. Something Heidi Finnischann had said to him the first time they'd met. Talking about the Schloss Luzvimmen cheese-making operation, she had told him that the cows were housed in what used to be dungeons. She had also told him that some people believed there were still some dungeons down there.

The memory refined his search.

Blotto's stomach rumbles were getting worse. Twinks had forbidden him from putting any of the cheese pellets into his mouth. But there still remained the furry toffee. Of course, if he did go for it, he would have to offer half. Indeed, to be a complete gentleman, he should offer the whole thing, secure in the knowledge that she, being the complete lady, would suggest cutting it in half.

His hand hovered over his jacket pocket.

Then dipped in and closed over a piece of paper. He pulled it out, not having a clue where it came from.

'What's that when it's got its spats on?' asked Twinks.

'Haven't got a mouse-squeak of an idea. It's all written in spoffing foreign.'

'Let me turn my truffler on to it, Blotters.'

As he handed across the flyer with images of skiers on it, he remembered taking it from the noticeboard in the cheese-processing works.

'It's about a skiing race . . .' Twinks pronounced.

'Is it, by Denzil?'

'... that's due to start ...' Twinks consulted the tiny silver watch in her sequined reticule '... in an hour's time. That's interesting.'

'Why, Twinkers? Nothing to do with us. No skin off my rice pudding.'

'What is interesting about it, Blotto me old antimacassar, is who the race is being contested by.'

Corky Froggett reckoned he'd found the area where the dungeons were. Except for the pillars which held up the huge weight of Schloss Luzvimmen, the whole underground space had been cleared to make room for holding pens and milking stations for the many cows. Three of the walls of the rectangle were lined with containers for churns, tools, hay and other fodder. The fourth was bare rock. But closer inspection showed the outline of three doors cut into the stone. They had no handles but three large keyholes.

Corky wished Twinks was beside him with the multi-functional picklocks from her sequined reticule, but no such luck. He felt pretty convinced, though, that she was very close to him, just the other side of one of the stone doors.

Corky Froggett reconciled himself, as he had so many times during his professional life, to waiting.

'Splendissimo!' said Twinks. 'It explains the whole clangdumble!'

'Does it?' asked Blotto dubiously.

'Is the King German?' asked Twinks rhetorically. 'It explains Sister Anneliese-Marie and Aurelia ffrench-

168

Windeau's "devotions" and straightens the corkscrew on the whole "Secret Order of the Slalomists" flipmadoodle!'

'Does it?' repeated Blotto, still unenlightened.

'Yes, it does – easy as raspberries!' She flourished the flyer in front of her brother. 'Clap your peepers on it!'

'It's still in spoffing foreign,' Blotto objected.

Twinks spelt it out for him. 'There's a slalom skiing race due to take place on the slopes of Luzvimmen at ten o'clock this morning. The two teams involved are from the Convent of the Sacred Icicle and the Convent of the Holy Temptation! That tickles your mustard, doesn't it?'

'Does it?' asked Blotto.

Corky Froggett had had longer waits. He'd once stayed in the Lagonda, while the young master enjoyed club claret in The Gren with a bunch of his Old Etonian muffin-toasters, for three days and nights. He never complained. They didn't make stuff sterner than what Corky Froggett was made of.

His hunch proved correct. Though he didn't know of Count von Strapp's plans for world domination, he did know why people got imprisoned. They were being kept for a purpose. They could somehow be of use to their captors. A man like the Count, whose powers and lack of moral values Heidi Finnischann had spelt out to him in her hayloft, would not hesitate to eliminate anyone who stood in his way. The fact that he was allowing Blotto and Twinks to live meant he hadn't finished with them yet.

So, he wouldn't want them to starve to death before they had fulfilled their function.

Corky saw a black-clad man detaching himself from the crowds of black-clad cowherds and milkmaids. The metal covers on the tray he carried were obviously covering plates of food.

He stopped facing one of the door shapes, put the tray down on the floor and pulled a large key out of his pocket.

The man certainly never knew what hit him. Corky Froggett had learnt many skills during the recent little dust-up in France, and was a highly efficient killing machine. In this instance, since he had nothing against the food-deliverer, he confined his skills to being a highly efficient immobilising machine. The victim would wake up in a couple of hours with a splitting headache and no recollection of what had happened to him.

The chauffeur took the key, slotted it into the lock and calmly opened the door ... to reveal Blotto and Twinks, who cried out in unison, 'Corky!'

'You really are the panda's panties!' said Blotto. 'You've brought us some spoffing comestibles! I could eat a horse – snaffle, stirrups and saddle!'

Twinks gathered up her sequined reticule, not bothering to take the Wilhelm Tell book with her, and cried out, 'Grandissimo! You really are the lark's larynx, Corky!'

She rushed past him and out of the Sealed Unit's door. 'I must get to the ski slopes!'

17

Well Off-Piste

None of the black-clad cowherds and milkmaids even noticed the slender Englishwoman rushing past them. In the staff changing room, Twinks divested herself of her Sylviane Heffelfinger costume and put on a spare nun's habit that, for some reason, was lying around.

Then she picked up a pair of skis. She had never tried that mode of transport before, but reasoned that, for someone with innate sporting instincts and a good sense of balance, it couldn't be too difficult.

Also, with skis on, she'd move more quickly over the snow to the start of the Convent of the Sacred Icicle v. the Convent of the Holy Temptation slalom race. She wasn't particularly concerned with the result – which team would actually be presented with the Holy Grail – but she did want some explanations from Sister Anneliese-Marie and Aurelia ffrench-Windeau.

She strapped the skis on to her feet. Picked up two poles and, with perfect poise, slid gracefully across the sparkling whiteness. To add to the beauty of the scene, snow had now begun to fall heavily.

* * *

Blotto had already sat down in the Sealed Unit's doorway and was removing the metal covers from the plates, before he noticed the reproachful look in his chauffeur's eye. 'Oh, Corkers,' he said, 'don't you think I should be stuffing the old tooth-box with the noshings?'

'I think it might be more appropriate at this moment,' said Corky Froggett respectfully, 'if you were to follow the young mistress. You may be out of your prison, but you are still on the premises of the people who locked you up in there.'

'Bong on the nose, Corky,' said Blotto, standing up with a wistful look at the tray of food. 'Yes, let's find these oikish sponge-worms and batter them from The Oval to Lord's via Edgbaston!'

It wasn't the oldest of the Lyminster family's war cries – that had been the full-throated – 'à bas les autres!' they'd used at the Battle of Hastings – but it had the right effect. Blotto set off at high speed for the staff entrance in pursuit of his sister, with a belligerent Corky Froggett in his wake.

As he ran, the chauffeur divested himself of his black overgarments, which he left in a pile in the changing room by the exit.

And there, to Blotto's ecstatic response, the guards had left his snowboarding cricket bat. The moment he grasped the familiar handle, he felt titanised. 'Come on, Corkers! Now we'll show the four-faced filchers what it's like to have Englishmen rattling their ribcages!'

Though none of the black-clad workers in the underground cow accommodation appeared to have taken any notice, there was a very efficient system of spying throughout

Schloss Luzvimmen. It did not take long for news of the escape from the Sealed Unit to get higher up the building. Ulrich Weissfeder was the first to be informed.

He immediately went down to inspect the scene of the crime.

Something he found there stabbed an icicle of fear through his heart. A very uncomfortable conversation with Count von Strapp lay ahead of him.

As she skied onwards with unthinking skill, Twinks felt she was getting close to achieving the mission that had brought her to Switzerland. She knew that the explanation of Aurelia ffrench-Windeau's situation was somehow involved with the slalom race between the two convents.

She checked in her mind what she knew about slalom. Developed in Norway during the nineteenth century, the rules for modern slalom were codified by Arnold Lunn for the British National Ski Championships in 1922. Basically, the competitor's aim was to complete a downhill course between gates of alternating red and blue poles in the shortest time possible.

It was clear, though, as she approached the start of the race, that the rules in Luzvimmen were more primitive. There were no poles planted in the snow, for a start. The skiers had to skirt round trees dotted around the slope. And also, the race was not judged by individual timed runs. As in a conventional running race, all of the contestants started at the same time. Which offered multiple opportunities for collisions.

Arriving at the start, Twinks became aware that the race was already under way. A group of nuns at the starting gate were watching the dwindling figures of four skiers, three in black habits and one in white, vanishing down the slope in the falling snow.

'Don't don your worry-boots!' Twinks shouted to the bewildered sisters. 'I'll bet a guinea to a groat that I can catch them up!'

'How dare you bring that thing in here!' From their position, seated behind the control room desk, the eyebrows bristled in fury. 'You will not escape my wrath this time, Weissfeder! The name that is not to be spoken must not be seen in printed material either! I think, Weissfeder, it is time for you to face your punishment on the Cheese Grater!'

'No! Please, Eure Exzellenz! Allow me to explain!' Ulrich Weissfeder sounded – and looked – terrified.

'The time for explanations is past! The time for the Cheese Grater has come! Guards!'

Instantly, four black-clad men were inside the room with them. The Count gestured to them to seize the unfortunate hotelier. Which they did.

'*No!*' Ulrich Weissfeder shrieked. 'It is important that I tell you where this book was found!'

'Oh?' The eyebrows wilted slightly.

'You know the two prisoners who were put in the Sealed Unit . . .'

'Of course I do!' the Count snapped back.

'Someone has released them.'

'That is not possible!'

'I'm afraid it is. And this book . . .' Weissfeder pointed at it '. . . was left in their empty cell.'

Even behind the eyebrows, one could see how pale the Count's face had become. 'No!' he said. 'No!'

174

Weissfeder pushed forward his advantage. 'I think it was a calling card for you.'

It was the Count's turn to shriek now, as he went on, 'Wilhelm Tell is inside Schloss Luzvimmen!'

'Jollissimo!' cried Twinks, as she glided in and out of the trees. 'This really is the panda's panties!'

Never had she felt such freedom of movement. Accelerating effortlessly, steering with only the slightest shifts of her bodyweight and the lightest touches of her poles, she felt the closest she'd ever been to flying.

And she was gaining quickly on the other competitors. As she flashed past two skiing nuns in black habits, she turned back to check their faces but didn't recognise either. Must be from the Convent of the Holy Temptation. Still ahead of her were one in black and one in white. They had to be Sister Anneliese-Marie and the one who was now called Sister Liselotte. The latter, with every second, was drawing further away from her teammate.

With a cheery wave, Twinks passed the Mother Superior. By now, the finishing line was in sight, attended by bunches of excited nuns.

Before she reached it, as she shot past Aurelia ffrench-Windeau, Twinks realised, in her inexperience, the one thing she didn't know about skiing.

How to stop.

From his control room, Count von Strapp could operate loudspeakers to sound out all over Schloss Luzvimmen. He addressed his black-clad guards through the microphone on his huge desk.

'We are going into action stations earlier than expected. The threat against us has already been unleashed. Your first task is to recapture the escaped English prisoners. They must be taken alive. Then I will have the enormous pleasure of watching them face the Cheese Grater.

'And, in the meantime, prepare for war! We must fight off the attacks of Wilhelm Tell!'

The whole massive building seemed to shudder. The unsayable had been said.

Count von Strapp had named the one whose name is not to be spoken.

Not knowing any other ways of stopping her descent, Twinks used the tried-and-tested method she often resorted to on toboggan runs at Tawcester Towers. She fell on to the ground.

Her momentum meant that she actually came to a halt some way further down the slope than she had fallen. And she found going uphill on skis a lot more difficult than going down.

As she approached the finishing line, she was surprised to see a bevy of excited nuns running towards her. One, who seemed to have some level of authority among them, was carrying a gold cup, which had some inscription in Swiss German engraved on it. She held the trophy out towards Twinks.

'You have won the Holy Grail,' she announced. 'Which convent do you represent?'

'Oh, Lordie in a kitchen coop!' said Twinks, selecting the right answer. 'I represent the Secret Order of the Slalomists!'

176

18

Well Piste-Off

By the time Blotto and Corky Froggett had exited Schloss Luzvimmen, Twinks was already out of sight in the falling snow, off on her inadvertent skiing race.

'Where to, milord?' asked the chauffeur.

'To the Lagonda!' cried the young master. 'We want to kick the ice of this fumacious gluepot off our heels as quick as a lizard's lick.'

'Isn't there anything else you need to do while we're out here, milord?' Corky's question was not completely altruistic. Though he had never expected his encounter with Heidi Finnischann to have any future, he would have liked to say a proper goodbye to her. After all, they hadn't met since she had been frightened off by the Two Avengers they had seen on the slopes the previous night. (Rationalising these apparitions with hindsight, he reckoned they probably must have been a couple of Holy Temptation nuns getting in a bit of last-minute practice for the race ahead.)

'Nothing that can't be knocked on the noodle,' Blotto replied to the question about things he needed to do. He did feel a bit guilty about not fulfilling his promise to Buffy 'Crocker' Wilmslow. He'd said he'd definitely get revenge on Victor Muke-Wallingborough by making Lewdie look like a coward. But that promise had been made before Count von Strapp started trying to coffinate him with cheeseballs.

No, for once in his life, Blotto would have to let discretion be the better part of valour.

'But we can't leave without the young mistress,' Corky objected.

'We'll pick the little droplet up on the way down,' said Blotto.

His chauffeur couldn't share his employer's confidence of how easy that would be, but his time in the military had insulated him from the thought of questioning an order from his superiors, so the two of them strode across the crisp surface towards the village.

The falling snow did not help visibility from Count von Strapp's control room, but he could see enough to tell the black-clad operatives behind the guns what to do. Blotto and Corky's dark clothing made them clear targets against the enveloping whiteness.

Ulrich Weissfeder watched on in fascinated excitement.

'Destroy them!' were the Count's orders. 'They are spies sent by Wilhelm Tell.'

'But, Eure Exzellenz,' suggested Weissfeder with diffidence, 'surely you don't want to destroy them yet. You want to recapture them, so that they can face the sentence of the Cheese Grater.'

'Good point, Weissfeder. Strange . . . every now and then you do come up with quite sensible ideas.'

'Thank you, Eure Exzellenz.' The hotelier squirmed with delight at the commendation.

'So, will that be large ammunition or small, sir?' asked one of the gunmen.

'Start with the large,' said the Count. 'That will immobilise them. Then, as Weissfeder suggests, we can pick them up and bring them back here to face the Cheese Grater.'

Following instructions, the two men loaded the rubbery balls into the breeches and looked along the sights of their gun barrels.

On the command of 'Fire!' from the Count, they squeezed the triggers.

Blotto heard the noise of the cheeseball thudding into the snow some fifty yards ahead of him. He watched, with shock but not surprise, as the yellow mass speedily expanded to the size of a small tent.

Another thud, some ten yards closer, still landing in front.

'Back towards the castle!' barked Corky Froggett, benefiting from all he'd learnt during the recent little dust-up in France. 'At this elevation, it's harder for them to resight on a target moving closer.'

Blotto didn't hesitate to do as he was told. He was never too proud to take advice from someone who knew more about a subject than he did. That was why he'd been taking instruction from Twinks about everything since the moment she was born.

Another cheeseball landed on a tree worryingly close to them. The way it spread down the branches, brushing off the snow and encasing everything in its glutinous embrace, showed just how easily it could stop a man in his tracks.

179

Their diverted route was now taking them away from the village. They didn't want to go too far towards the Schloss, because of the risk of recapture. Corky pointed towards the Croissant Run clubroom. 'Make our way over there, milord! It'll give us some protection!'

Twinks had seen her brother and Corky out on the slopes and made her way to join them, now able to manage her skis better on the horizontal plane. As she glided along, she too became aware of the cheeseballs detonating around her.

She recognised them for what they were – devices designed to entrap rather than kill. She knew the situation would become a lot more dangerous when the Count and his troops started using the smaller pellets.

She must protect Blotto and Corky from that moment.

'They're making for the start of the Croissant Run, Eure Exzellenz!' announced Ulrich Weissfeder, scanning the slopes through binoculars.

'Good,' said Count von Strapp savagely. 'That makes things much easier for us. If they go inside for shelter, we'll have a fixed target to attack.' He addressed the men at the guns. 'Suspend firing until I give the order to restart! And set your sights on the start of the Croissant Run!'

Twinks had caught up with the two men before they reached the clubhouse. She was still clutching the Holy Grail. Sadly, it was one of the few things too big to fit into her sequined reticule.

'Beezer to see you, sis!' said Blotto enthusiastically. 'From now on, we'll be rolling on camomile lawns. The lumps of toadspawn have given up trying to hit us with their horracious cheeseballs.'

'I wouldn't be so sure about that, Blotto me old nostril-hair-remover. Don't count your blue tits before they're born.'

'Everything's going to be creamy éclair,' he responded breezily. 'Just you wait and see. Then into the Lag and non-stop pongling back to Tawcester Towers!'

'Rein in the roans a moment there,' said Twinks.

'What's put lumps in your custard, Twinkers?'

'I came out to Switzerland to find out what had happened to Berry ffrench-Windeau's little droplet of a sister. Well, I've now found out what shape of ball she's playing with, but I still need to sort out the to-dos on getting her back to the Land of the Golden Lions.'

'Can't that wait?' pleaded Blotto.

'No, it spoffing well cannot wait!' His sister had suddenly turned one hundred and ten per cent Dowager Duchess.

Blotto might have argued further, but they were interrupted by the earth-shaking thud of a projectile landing only feet away from them.

'Quick, inside the clubhouse, milord and milady!' urged Corky Froggett. 'Take shelter!'

'Wait till they're safely inside,' Count von Strapp gave orders to his gunmen, 'then start with the other ammunition.'

'The pellets?' one of the guards asked.

181

'No, the conventional weaponry first,' said the Count with one of his best evil smiles. 'Then the pellets.'

Their entrance brought sudden silence to the clubhouse. Brandy glasses were suspended in mid-air, pipes fell from unclenching jaws, chins (many of which hardly existed) dropped.

The fact was, never before had a woman been seen in the place. It wasn't Twinks's exquisite beauty that silenced them. It was just her gender.

'Now, listen, me old muffin-toasters!' said Blotto. 'We may be in a bit of a treacle tin here. The fumacious slug-buckets up in Schloss Luzvimmen are bombarding us with the most devilish of military ammo!'

'What ammo?' asked a contemptuous Lewdie.

'Cheeseballs,' Blotto replied.

The roar of derision which greeted this was instantly stilled as Twinks spoke. 'Don't get your giggle-boots on about it. This is the most advanced development in weaponry since the Accrington-Murphy machine gun.'

Corky Froggett found this claim unlikely, but he knew it was not the right moment to contradict the young mistress. (Indeed, it was never the right moment to contradict the young mistress.)

Victor Muke-Wallingborough wasn't convinced either. 'Listen, doll,' he sneered, deliberately placing the diminishing insult. 'I've never been afraid of anything in my entire life and, if you think I'm going to be scared of cheese, I suggest you go back to your boudoir and get on with your embroidery.'

Blotto seethed inwardly. Lewdie was adding insulting his sister to many other offences. There must be a way revenge could be achieved on Crocker's behalf. But, at that moment, he couldn't see what it was.

'Just take my word for it,' said Twinks coolly, not rising to Lewdie's gibes, 'all of you. We are in a horracious gluepot and will need Lucifer's own luck to get out of it!'

As if to reinforce her words, the ceiling of the clubhouse suddenly fell in. Count von Strapp's 'conventional weaponry' – old-fashioned stone cannonballs – had scored two direct hits.

As the dust and debris started to settle, Twinks became aware of rubbery cheeseballs raining down through the absent roof.

'Everyone skiddle out of here,' she cried, 'quick as a lizard's lick! They're sending in the heavy cheese!'

The various muffin-toasters left their pipes and brandy glasses (and would have left their chins if they'd had any) in an ungainly scramble for the exit.

Only one stood firm. With a supercilious smile, he said, 'The day that Victor Muke-Wallingborough is frightened of cheese is the day that will never come!'

Twinks's instinct was right. They were – at least, temporarily – safer outside the clubhouse. The gunmen in Schloss Luzvimmen had not had time to adjust their sights and continued to rain rubbery cheeseballs into the building.

The attention of the confused crowd on the snow was suddenly drawn to a clubhouse window. In it appeared the anguished face of Victor Muke-Wallingborough. At his back, pressing him against the glass, was an expanding wall of yellow.

'Help!' he cried. 'Somebody rescue me! I'm so frightened! I'm scared of—'

183

But his words – and his body – were swallowed by the swelling cheese.

There was a ladder against the clubhouse wall. Blotto mounted it, cricket bat in hand and cried, 'I'm going to save the spoffing coward!'

Twinks, Corky and the assembled muffin-toasters watched in appalled silence as the rescuer broke the window glass with his cricket bat and pushed himself into the gooey mass which, now released, started spilling down the outside of the clubhouse.

Twinks and Corky, who had infinite confidence in Blotto's ability to achieve anything that didn't involve thinking, were at first untroubled. But, as expanding cheese began to spill out of the shattered roof, and the invisibility of Blotto and Lewdie continued, both of them felt flutterings of concern.

The Old Etonian muffin-toasters around them were less sanguine. Mutterings about 'couple of fine boddoes ...', 'Blotto's double century in the Eton and Harrow match will never be forgotten ...' and 'come to us all in time ...' increased in volume. The amateur obituarists were already at work.

Then, as the awful reality of the situation made its impression, the mutterings dropped to silence. The bombardment from the Schloss Luzvimmen control room had also ceased. The only sound was the soft rustle of snow falling.

The silence extended too far to leave room for hope. No human being could survive in the choking goo of cheese for so long.

Then, suddenly, there was movement from the club-house's clogged doorway. The cheese filling it bulged like a blister, then burst to reveal a triumphant Blotto, one hand on his cricket bat and the other leading a whimpering Victor Muke-Wallingborough, whose eyes were firmly closed, out of danger. Both men were covered in molten cheese.

'How on earth did you do it, milord?' asked a flabbergasted Corky Froggett.

Twinks knew the answer, but she let her brother have his moment.

'It was as easy as a housemaid's virtue,' said Blotto. 'Simply a matter of pongling one's way from one air pocket to the other. You see,' he added with pride, 'if there was one thing I knew for certain, it was that the spoffing cheese would have holes in it!'

This statement, with its implication of tactical planning by Blotto, was greeted by huge cheers from the assembled muffin-toasters.

The noise was sufficient to make Lewdie open his eyes.

'Am I all right?' he asked in a feeble voice. 'Is the ordeal over? Oh, I've never been so frightened in my life!'

'Don't don your worry-boots about it,' said Twinks gently. 'Even the bravest of us have moments of cowardice.'

'But who saved me?' Lewdie looked around the assembled throng in bewilderment. Had he had his wits about him, he would have identified the only other person present who was covered in cheese.

Blotto was too modest to claim the honour but his sister answered the question.

'I can never thank you enough, Lyminster,' said Lewdie.

'I didn't do it for myself,' said Blotto. 'I did it for Crocker.'

Victor Muke-Wallingborough shrank into the awareness of his shame. Having been so publicly revealed as a coward, in a scenario played out in front of all his muffin-toasters, he would never regain the status he had once had amongst them.

Twinks, however, was aware that the danger from Schloss Luzvimmen was not over. 'We must split up!' she cried. 'Together, we're too big a target, as obvious as a kitten in a basket of puppies. Come on, put a jumping cracker under it!'

'But surely,' said one optimistic muffin-toaster, 'now we know the expanding cheeseballs have holes in them, we're not in so much danger.'

'Don't stake your shimmy on that!' Twinks responded, before giving him a very quick report on the scientific experiments she'd conducted in the Sealed Unit. 'Count von Strapp has another, more deadly, form of ammunition. Small pellets – and you'll be kippered like a herring to hear . . . they expand into a cheese which doesn't have any holes in it. What's more, they expand on a much bigger scale than the ones they've just pumped into the clubhouse. And what makes them expand is the tidgiest touch of water. So, if one were to land on someone with snow on their shoulders, the snow would melt, cause the expansion, encase the victim in impermeable cheese, and coffinate him within seconds!'

As if in illustration of her words, something appeared to hit Corky Froggett, who was standing right next to her. Twinks watched in horror as, instantly melting the snow on his shoulders, the pellet expanded at terrifying speed.

Within seconds, the chauffeur's whole body was encased in a carapace of hard cheese.

186

19

Facing the Cheese Grater

It was fortunate that Twinks's scientific experiments in the Sealed Unit had also investigated the means of counteracting the cheese pellets' murderous potential. As in so many human situations of stress, alcohol worked wonders.

The moment she saw Corky immobilised, Twinks had her sequined reticule open and was unstoppering the brandy bottle. But, as she did so, she registered an unwelcome sight. Thundering down the slopes towards them on skis, a posse of Count von Strapp's black-clad guards emerged from the falling snow.

Twinks dripped a little brandy on to the cheese which covered the chauffeur's mouth. 'Just so's you can breathe, Corkers,' she whispered. 'Then I'll make a crack so's you can escape.'

She trickled a line of brandy down the side of his cheesy prison. There was a slight sizzling sound as the alcohol burnt through.

'But I'm going to tip your topple first.' Matching action to words, she pushed over the solid figure and turned the body so that the crack she'd made wasn't visible. 'Lie doggo, Corky. I want them to think they've coffinated you.'

'Very good, milady,' he hissed through the alcohol-bored aperture. The muffled voice quality did not allow Twinks to recognise the disappointment in his tone. Yet again, he had been frustrated in his attempts to lay down his life for the young master and the young mistress. And this time, he'd been really close.

The skirmish between the Old Etonians and the Count's black-clad guards was brief. In different circumstances, the assembled muffin-toasters might have organised a more effective resistance, but they were out of sorts and cowed by the bewildering sequence of events they had just witnessed.

And, in spite of a valiant rearguard action by Blotto and his cricket bat, superior numbers told once again. Soon, he and his sister were recaptured and on their way back to Schloss Luzvimmen.

'You have escaped me before,' said the Count with evil satisfaction, 'but this time you are mine for good. For good, but not for long. Reveal the Cheese Grater!'

Ulrich Weissfeder, with obsequious gratification, pulled a lever. A large part of the control room's back wall slid aside to reveal a vertical row of rollers like giant bicycle chains. They moved alternately in opposite directions, the chains armed with saw-teeth. There was a narrowing tray sticking out into the room, clearly what was used to feed in the material for grating.

Unlike everything else in the Chäs Luzvimmen operation, the tray was not sparkling clean. It had been deliberately left stained with old blood.

Neither Blotto nor Twinks doubted that the blood was human.

Count von Strapp seemed to take their understanding of the situation as read. 'Yes,' he purred. 'A very effective way of disposing of people who become too difficult. And you two, I'm afraid ... "Blotto" and "Twinks" shall I call you ... have become far too difficult. I'm afraid, when you decided to work for Wilhelm Tell, you made a bad decision. A very bad decision. You went for the wrong side.'

The aristocratic siblings were both held hard by black-clad guards. Blotto could see his cricket bat pleading to him from the other side of the room. But there was no way, even with his strength, that he could break free of his captors and secure it.

Twinks knew that her sequined reticule was safe under her garments but, in her pinioned state, she would have a hard job to access it. Worming her fingers down very slowly, she tried to reach the clasp.

'You may worry,' the Count went on, very confident now, all paranoia gone, 'about the effect the admixture of grated human remains has on the quality of Chäs Luzvimmen. Well, let me set your minds at rest. We manufacture here on such a scale that, once ground-up body parts reach the churning vats, they are quickly over-whelmed by the quantity of pure cheese. Extensive tests down at our works at the foot of the mountain have shown no discernible trace of non-vegetable matter in the finished product.

'So, once you have been through the Cheese Grater ... *Blotto and Twinks* ...' he lingered irritatingly over the names '... you will effectively have ceased to exist.'

189

'You can't make a Lyminster cease to exist!' said Blotto defiantly. 'The family spirit has survived the Norman Conquest, the Wars of the Roses, the English Civil—'

'Gag him!' came the order. Which the guards efficiently did.

'And I think we have had enough time-wasting now,' the Count resumed. 'Feed these two into the Cheese Grater, while I get on with something more important.'

'And what's that "something more important" when it's got its spats on?' asked Twinks coolly.

'It is defeating my sworn enemy,' the Count replied. 'Which will be very easily done.'

He gestured to the weaponry around him. There were serried ranks of open ammunition boxes, some featuring the large cheeseballs, others the deadlier pellets. There was also a pile of the old-fashioned stone cannonballs.

'No one can resist these armaments!' he cried. 'With what I have developed here at Schloss Luzvimmen, I am already the most powerful commander in the whole of Europe, probably the whole of the world!

'But, before I go for world domination, I have to deal with a minor local annoyance. I have to defeat Wilhelm Tell!'

'I think you might have a bijou problemette there,' Twinks observed dispassionately.

'Oh yes? And what do you mean by that?'

'I mean by that, my dear Count, that it is hard to defeat an enemy . . .' She took a dramatic pause before her revelation '. . . *who does not exist.*'

The eyebrows quivered, as if the face behind them had just received a heavy blow.

'Don't talk such nonsense! Of course, Wilhelm Tell exists!'

'No,' came the cool response. 'Probably never has existed.'

190

'How can you say that?'

'With great ease. Wilhelm Tell – or William Tell – was a folk myth originating in the fifteenth century. There is no historical proof he ever existed. And he has certainly not been reincarnated in the twentieth century.'

'He exists,' Count von Strapp protested feebly.

'No. Allow me to elucidate. I'm not sure if you are aware of the fascinating recent research by the well-known bonkers-doctor Sigmund Freud into the human unconscious. He would definitely have a name for the psychosis you are suffering from, Count von Strapp. Or, if he hasn't encountered it before, perhaps he would allow you the honour of donating your name to it. The Von Strapp Complex?

'You see, what you are doing with all your talk of Wilhelm Tell is sublimating your fears of the evil side of your own identity by giving them human form. To reconcile your own duality, you have created an evil alter-ego, in the hope of finding in the "cleansed" part of yourself a personality you can live with. Wilhelm Tell does not exist outside your own imagination. You cannot possibly defeat him, because, as I said before, he does not exist!'

Blotto was finding all of this a bit confusing. He didn't know what the sis was cluntering on about, and he thought an easier cashew to crunch might be suspending the sermon and finding the fisticuffs.

But, though Twinks's words didn't touch her brother, the effect they were having on Count von Strapp was devastating. The eyebrows quivered, shuddered and shook. From behind them, tears could be seen glinting in the eyes of the aspiring world dominator. In one of the quickest sessions of psychotherapy ever recorded, Twinks

191

had identified the patient's psychosis and dismantled his *raison d'être*. The Count had been psychologically destroyed.

But, still, secure in his private arsenal, surrounded by black-clad guards, with the Cheese Grater whirring nearby, he remained a threat to his prisoners. Twinks knew she had to do something about the situation.

Fortunately, she had now wriggled her fingers inside her sequined reticule. Blessing her foresight in packing them, she produced one of the self-igniting fireworks. She threw it up in the air, where it self-ignited, detonating an enormous flash which stunned everyone present.

In that moment of shock, the two prisoners shook free of their captors' restraining arms. 'Cannonball, Blotters!' shouted Twinks. 'Lob it at the spoffing window!'

As always, he did precisely what his sister told him to. As the impact of the massive stone shivered the glass in front of them, Twinks had already extracted two silken cords from her sequined reticule and affixed them to the base of one of the guns.

Grabbing one of them herself and passing the other to her brother, she cried out, 'Off we go, Blotters! Zippetty-split!'

And, with a hearty 'Jollissimo!' trailing behind them, Blotto and Twinks abseiled down the side of Schloss Luzvimmen to freedom.

Freedom, however, was not an experience to be shared by those who remained in the control room. The shattering of the window had allowed the snow to come in. Settling on the ammunition boxes, it melted. The thawed water activated the pellets and, within seconds, the entire space was filled with hard cheese.

The pressure this created burst though the control room

doors and the gooey mess spread across floors and down staircases.

Until the entire interior of Schloss Luzvimmen was one block of solid cheese.

At the foot of the castle walls, Blotto and Twinks nipped into dungeon-level changing rooms to find more suitable clothes for the next part of their escape. Twinks whipped off her nun's habit and put on a woollen cardigan and trousers. She wrapped a scarf around her neck and acquired a pair of sunglasses.

Blotto felt a pang at leaving his late father's suit behind, but recognised he'd never get all the cheese out of the thick tweed. He grabbed trousers, jumper, scarf and woollen hat. Sunglasses, too, like his sister.

They also both picked up and strapped on skis.

Blotto, who had never been near a pair before, of course managed to use them instinctively. As they smoothed their way down the slope, the snow stopped falling. Sister Anneliese-Marie had appeared from somewhere and was skiing along behind them.

They had a moment of anxiety when three black-clad figures on skis also joined the trail. But it soon became clear that the men were not pursuing them. They were skiing for their lives to escape the encroaching cheese, which was taking over all of Schloss Luzvimmen.

'Grandissimo!' exulted Twinks, as the sun, glowing through the clouds, added a crisp radiance to the Alpine scene. 'Isn't everything just creamy éclair!'

20

Fondue Memories

Despite the huge power he had exercised over Luzvimmen, Count von Strapp was not missed at all. Nor was Ulrich Weissfeder. And all the villagers who had worked for Chäs Luzvimmen survived the destruction of the Schloss. Because they only dealt with the cows at the dungeon level, they had time to evacuate the premises, with their mooing charges, before the fatal tide of cheese arrived.

It was soon agreed that the local cheesemaking operation would be continued, but on a much smaller scale, under the management of the Convent of the Sacred Icicle. In time, Chäs Luzvimmen would become respected as a rather special artisan cheese brand, with no aspirations to be the biggest in the whole of Europe, probably the whole of the world.

Though, in time, delicatessens all over the world would stock and charge ridiculous prices for it.

Blotto, Twinks and Corky Froggett no longer felt such inordinate urgency to return to Tawcester Towers.

Christmas was approaching and the arguments in favour of not being home for the festival remained as persuasive as ever.

As a result, Corky got to spend more time in Heidi Finnischann's hayloft. Having been reassured as to the identity of the two skiers who had so spooked her at night on the mountainside, she relaxed into her normal easy personality. The loss of her employment up at the Schloss caused her no regret. She would just spend more time with the family cows, and also develop her skills as a language teacher and ski instructor. The winter-sports boom was all set to take over in Luzvimmen.

Heidi and Corky both knew they would have to part soon, but neither of them let that stop them enjoying their exchange of blandishments.

Buffy 'Crocker' Wilmslow made a good recovery from his second leg break. (Blotto even made rather a good joke about the double meaning of 'leg break', as an injury and a kind of ball bowled at cricket. His friend found the joke very funny at least the first seven times he was told it.)

Crocker was soon back on the (repaired) Croissant Run, though this time he did pay a little more attention to Doktor Krankenschwindler's strictures. Given the good fortune of possessing two unbroken arms, Crocker thought he'd quite like to keep things that way.

And, of course, he was now able to lord it in the club-room. Victor Muke-Wallingborough was reduced to a pale shadow of his former self. Though his fellow muffin-toasters weren't unpleasant to him, as someone who had displayed cowardice, he would never recapture his invincible aura. Nobody called him 'Lewdie' any more.

The idea of him coming out the winner in any sporting contest had become vaguely ludicrous.

The change of status affected his results, too. His chalked-up times were never near the top of the black-board any more. That place belonged to Devereux Lyminster, who continued to lower the record with virtually every run.

Blotto also built on his brief experience of skiing and was soon beating everyone else at that, too.

Maybe, he ruminated, he'd been too dismissive of winter sports. In the short time they remained in Luzvimmen, there was nothing he enjoyed more, with his equally skilled sister by his side, than gliding down ever more challenging slopes.

Twinks, of course, still had unfinished business in Luzvimmen. Though bringing down the evil empire of Count von Strapp was a satisfactory achievement, it wasn't what she had travelled to Switzerland for. The case of Aurelia ffrench-Windeau still needed further explanation.

Twinks's reception at the Convent of the Sacred Icicle was more welcoming this time. After all, although she wasn't technically a member of the institution, she had recently won the Holy Grail for them. And, by doing so, got one over on the Convent of the Holy Temptation, their bitterest rivals.

When making the arrangements for this visit, Twinks had made clear that she didn't want Sister Benedicta or Sister Dagmar or any of the other nuns present. Just Sister Anneliese-Marie and Aurelia ffrench-Windeau. (Twinks was damned if she was going to call the girl 'Sister Liselotte'.)

When the three were seated in the Mother Superior's office, a novice brought in a fondue set. A metal pot over a burning flame, sliced chunks of bread and wooden skewers. The girl left and each of the three had a rewarding dip into the molten cheese before Twinks embarked on what she wanted to say.

'Look, I don't want to fiddle round the fir trees, but I do want to know what, in the name of ginger, is going on?'

'In what connection?' asked Sister Anneliese-Marie.

'You know spoffing well in what connection! All this gubbins about "devotions". All this "Secret Order of the Slalomists" toffee.'

'It is not toffee,' said the affronted Mother Superior. 'It is divinely ordained.'

'By whom?'

'When one uses the word "divinely",' came the acid response, 'one is usually referring to God.'

'So, where in the scriptures which, I've been told since I was in nursery-naps, are the word of God, does he give any specific advice about skiing?'

'It is not as literal as that. God speaks in metaphors.'

'Does he?' Twinks turned to Berry's sister. 'Do you speak in metaphors, Aurelia?'

The girl looked at her Mother Superior, possibly for permission. If so, she was denied it. She said nothing.

'Shall I tell you what I think has twisted up this corkscrew?' asked Twinks.

'I'd be interested to hear your opinion,' said Sister Anneliese-Marie. Though she didn't sound very interested.

'How long have you known you were going to become a nun, Sam?'

'As long as I can remember. It was the future my parents always wanted for me.'

'And how long was it the future you wanted for yourself?'

The Mother Superior coloured slightly as she replied, 'For the same length of time. From the moment I could understand what my parents were telling me.'

'"Telling" you. That's an interesting choice of words.'

'I meant "advising",' came the hasty correction.

'Well, I'll be jugged like a hare,' said Twinks. 'So, you were brought up, from the cradle and cot, to devote your life to God?'

'I love God.'

'I'm sure you do. Admirable boddo, does a lot of good gubbins round the place. But what happened, Sam, when you found something else to love, apart from God?'

The colour deepened. 'I've never found anything else to love. No man has ever touched my heart in the way that—'

'I'm not talking about amorous swains, Sam. I'm talking about spoffing skiing.' There was a silence. 'Can you deny that you love skiing as much as a pike loves troutlings?' The silence endured. 'Do you know what I think declogs the incog in this sit?'

'No,' came the quiet reply.

'Way it pops up to my peepers, Sam, is that, the moment you first encountered skiing, you fell for it like a guardsman in a heatwave. But that might tickle up potential conflict with your religious vocation. And the only way you could rigidify the rectangle on the problemette was to make your love of skiing a part of your religious observances. Which is why you invented the Secret Order of the Slalomists and all the other flipmadoodles!

'And why you invented all these strange rituals – with their own language, for the love of strawberries! The only way you could allow skiing into your life was to make it part of your religious vocation.'

Sister Anneliese-Marie's subdued reaction told Twinks all she needed to know. 'I think I've pinged the partridge there, Sam.'

Still receiving no response, Twinks turned back to the girl. 'And I think the same feather tickled your chin, Aurelia.'

'How do you mean?'

'The first time you clapped your peepers on skiing, you too fell for it like a guardsman in a heatwave.'

"That's true. I loved it! I knew I could do it. It was the first thing I ever knew I could be good at. Well, except for sex,' she said, just to balance things out.

'And,' Twinks continued, 'because it was out here in Luzvimmen that you had your first encounter . . .'

Aurelia looked puzzled. 'No, it wasn't. That was way back behind the cycle sheds at—'

'Your first encounter with *skiing*,' said Twinks.

'Oh yes, right. It was. That was out here.'

'And you desperately wanted to ski with every cell in your soul. Skiing became the first tick on your to-do. And the only way you could see to clock it on the calendar was to follow your Mother Superior's devotional route.'

'You're right!' cried Aurelia. 'That's exactly it. Sam is the best skiing coach there ever was. And if, to take advantage of those skills, I was going to have to go through all the Secret Order of the Slalomists nonsense, well, that was all right by me!'

'There was no other way I could do it!' Sister Anneliese-Marie cried out. 'I had never seen anyone with such natural talent for skiing. I had to harness that, train her on the wheeled practice boards before we got out onto the snow. First, I had to train her for the race against the Convent of the Holy Temptation, but later for much higher goals. There is now a real chance that soon women's Alpine skiing will be included in the Winter Olympics.

'With that possibility in mind, I knew I had to train Aurelia, to reach her full potential as the best slalomist in the world. And the only way I could do that, within my own vows as a nun, was by presenting it as a religious vocation!

'All that matters, you see, is that the unique skiing talents of Aurelia ffrench-Windeau are developed to the highest standards possible!'

Though she couldn't share the woman's logic, Twinks still felt gratified at having worked out her motivation. After Count von Strapp, that was the second accurate personality diagnosis she'd produced recently. Maybe she should give up on the sleuthing wodjermabit and develop her skills as a psychologist . . . ?

Aurelia ffrench-Windeau looked with pride at her mentor. Though the Mother Superior was clearly confused, it was a moment of bonding.

'Now, Sam,' said Twinks, 'are you beginning to turn the cloud round and see the silver? Life isn't a Roman road. You can squiggle with the wiggles, take diversions. It's quite possible to love God and to love skiing.'

'Is it?' asked the bewildered nun. It was the first time such a thought had been allowed access to her mind.

'Yes, it is, by Denzil,' said Twinks.

And that did it, really. Once Sister Anneliese-Marie realised that she could love God and skiing, she started questioning herself about which she loved more. And, though she always retained some affection for the Almighty, it was skiing that won.

She gave up her vocation at the Convent of the Sacred Icicle and became a full-time ski instructor. Her star pupil was Aurelia ffrench-Windeau.

And at the 1936 Winter Olympics at Garmisch-Partenkirchen, the first occasion on which women were allowed to participate in the combined (downhill and slalom) skiing event, Aurelia ffrench-Windeau was awarded the gold medal.

(Unfortunately, this result was subsequently changed, due to a technical disqualification. Because she had trained in Switzerland, Aurelia had been entered for the Swiss team. When she was found to be a British national, the medal was taken away and awarded to the athlete who had come a long way second to her in both disciplines. So, the record books now give the gold medal to the German skier, Christl Franziska Antonia Cranz-Borchers. But nobody who had been present at Garmisch-Partenkirchen in 1936 was left in any doubt that Aurelia ffrench-Windeau was the better athlete.)

Sam was much happier as a skiing coach than she had been as a Mother Superior.

And she did still go to church on Sundays, to show God there were no hard feelings.

The Phantom Skiers, incidentally, remained immured in the glacier at the Convent of the Sacred Icicle. When, decades later, global warming caused the ice to melt, there was no trace of them.

They had never been more than a trick of the light.

*   *   *

The journey in the Lagonda to Tawcester Towers was uneventful. Blotto, Twinks and Corky Froggett arrived back safely after Christmas. The Dowager Duchess was delighted (not that they were back, of course, just that she hadn't had to have them for the holiday season).

As it turned out, they could have made it to the ancestral home in time for the festivities. They arrived back in the Land of the Golden Lions on Christmas Eve. But, since nobody at Tawcester Towers knew about that, the siblings had booked into their customary London billet, the Savoy Hotel, and enjoyed all of the seasonal delights that the Savvers could offer.

When they did finally arrive in Tawcestershire, round Twelfth Night, Twinks had a brainwave. She showed her mother the Holy Grail and told her that it was the Biddability Cup she had mentioned before, the trophy awarded to the most submissive of the mature finishing school pupils.

The Dowager Duchess, who, with no knowledge of Swiss German, couldn't read the inscription, was delighted. A more biddable daughter had been her dream for many years. Now, she thought – mistakenly, as it turned out – that getting Twinks married off would be a whole lot easier.

The three of them, Twinks, Berengaria and Aurelia ffrench-Windeau, were sitting in the No Sympathy Bar of The Lady Graduates' Club. Eudoria Haggis had just served their cocktails.

It was Aurelia's first Suffra-Jet. It wouldn't be her last.